in the
Aftermath
of an
Overdose

Eleanore Hill

BETA BOOKS

In the Aftermath of an Overdose © 2014 Beta Books

an imprint of Mudborn Press ISBN 978-0-692289082

LITERARY FICTION

The Marty Trilogy—Eleanore Hil Aurora Leigh, E.B. Browning
Hadji Murad, Tolstoy The Basement, Newborn The First
Detective. Poe Matilda, Mary Shelley

SPECULATIVE FICTION

Frankenstein, Mary Shelley The Martian Testament, Newborn

HISTORY

Mitos y Leyendas/Myths and Legends of Mexico. Bilingual
Beechers Through the 19th Century Uncle Tom's Cabin, Stowe

SCHOOLING

Don't Panic: Procrastinator's Guide to Writing an Effective Term
Paper First Person Intense Italian for Opera Lovers
French for Food Lovers Doctorese for the imPatient

SPRITUAL

Ghazals of Ghalib Gandhi on the *Bhagavad Gita*
Gospel According to Tolstoy Everlasting Gospel, William Blake

LOVE

Dante & His Circle Vita Nuova Sappho Venus & Adonis

STAGING SHAKESPEARE

DIRECTOR'S PLAYBOOK SERIES: Hamlet Merchant of Venice
Twelfth Night Taming of the Shrew Midsummer Night's Dream Romeo
and Juliet As You Like It Richard III Henry V Much Ado About Nothing
Macbeth Othello Julius Caesar King Lear Antony and Cleopatra

7 Plays with Transgender Characters Falstaff: 4 Plays

TEACHER TEXTS

Areopagitica Apology of Socrates Leaves of Grass Sappho

www.bandannabooks.com college texts

www.betabooks.us ARCs, limited editions

in the
AFTERMATH
of an
OVERDOSE

AND YOU'RE JUST FINE, lying there as if asleep, with almost a smile on your sealed lips. But there's your mother answering the phone. It's the Consulate from Sydney, Australia. He tells her you are dead.

YOUR MOTHER IS IN DISBELIEF. She thinks it must be a joke. She asks how they know, and takes the detail with an open face. Listening as if to a story about someone else. You can see your mother's face as she stands there holding the cordless phone whose cradle sits there on that cupboard by the kitchen nook. The same phone you called from when you wanted drugs. There she is, a small woman, who bore you forty-three years ago. Grey but with a brown rinse to cover it, short, Italian, wrinkled. Seventy-eight. And this is how you treat her. You overdose and die, and she takes the news cold turkey, the first to answer the phone, while your father cocks an ear. He is just home from the Club. The Elks and then the Athletic Club. Your mother was in the middle of preparing dinner. It's four o'clock. The apartment smells like home, basil, garlic, warmth emanating from her little kitchen. She's making pasta, steamed vegetables, salad. In that little apartment kitchen she complains about because of lack of counter and cupboard space. She was just going along performing her duties, thinking about you over there on the other side of the earth. There's an envelope full of clippings she's been cutting out, jokes and articles, pictures of the flood, and news about the O.J. trial, she was ready to send. She was looking forward to talking to you when you called on Valentine's Day. That was the plan. She'd catch up on all your news. A mother's heart. And the calls were expensive. Forty-five minutes for forty-five dollars. But she loved those calls. Lived for them. She did her rosary beads and prayed to St. Jude. She stood silent when your last call said you'd gotten an extension on your stay. You got another six months. She figured if you were happy over there, that you knew what you were doing and she was happy for you. She smiled over your ability to persuade United to extend your ticket without increasing the rate. Six months more. You'd be home in June. She would have a big reunion. And your father's eightieth birthday would be celebrated, too.

SHE LOOKED FORWARD to your return. You were the light of her life she told people at the funeral. She just lit up when you entered the room. She used to laugh with you, unlike your father and older brother. That was all seriousness. Those two. You were the second and her last baby. Born five years after Matt. And now this. This is how you reward your mother. You only wanted that high. You only had thoughts of the next fix. You figured your mother would always be there and you could go ahead and think of yourself. Of course, it is the Me Generation, as your mother would soon be heard saying, in anguish, shaking her head at society and how it had changed from when she was your age."

NOW SHE HANDS THE PHONE to your father mumbling something about the Consulate calling from Australia and saying *Billy is dead.* Her voice is grave. Your father takes the phone, frowning hard, like a man, an Italian man, a Sicilian. His voice is gruff as he asks *what this is all about. What do you mean dead.* And then he bends into himself and awful sounds come out, like choking, while your mother looks on. She takes his cue. Then it's true. If Bill heard the same thing and isn't arguing, then it's true. Billy is dead. Your mother begins to whimper. Tiny frail little helpless sounds to your father's choking sounds. They look at each other. It has finally come to pass. Your death is what they were actively trying to avoid for twenty years. They'd watched you go through withdrawals so many times. They left it up to Matt, your big brother to do something to save you. They worried about you all the time. Only when you sat with them in the evenings, when you moved back in with them, after you lost your place when your roommates discovered you used drugs, did they know that you were alright. But, as soon as you were out of sight, their worry continued. Would you or wouldn't you come home. Or would they get a call. And now they got the call they'd feared since your were fifteen. You were dead at forty-three. And you were far away from home. This was the furthest you had ever traveled. Australia. But, they'd consoled themselves, you were with Ralph. Kind of under his care. He would surely let them know if your behavior showed any signs of drug abuse. And he'd never called. He had simply said for you to go home when he left for India.

HE TOLD MATT that when the family called about your dog dying. They were afraid you couldn't take the dog's death. They called Ralph and told him first, and that he was to keep an eye on you after they broke the bad news to you. They were afraid your grief would throw you into a relapse of needing to deaden your feelings. That you'd not be able to take the news so far away from home and alone. Little did they know your resources were social. A letter came from a young woman telling how she consoled you, exchanged poetry and prose pieces with you over death in general, and specifically your dog. Old Frankie was fourteen. A dog forced to be a vegetarian. And you, a silly owner, who tossed him an apple at whim and went off without noticing when the ribs were showing and the eyes were beginning to sink in. Without a lick of common sense about you, you contributed to your dog's demise, by starving him to death slowly for a three year period. Yes, his coat was beautiful. When you walked him, people saw that beautiful black and while silky border collie coat and complimented you. So how could you know the dog was suffering. You weren't that kind of guy. You were a city guy. A dog was a dog. You went by the book. If there was one book written by some ancient vegetarian that listed diets for dogs that didn't include meat, you'd go for it. You believed in the written manuals. You practiced Yoga that way. The handbook style with a marker at the page of the day. The saying of the day. The practice of the hour. The cliche and platitude of the moment. And the realness of your dog was just another abstraction. You could do your dog's life by number. Number one, cut up a cucumber, etc. Your brother's girlfriend lectured you about this, while you and Matt smiled to yourselves. What did she know. She was a ranter, is all. And then Frankie got that swelling in his prostrate. And you followed the vets *How to treat it by steps* method. The testicles had to be removed. He never said a thing about giving the dog what the dog wanted, meat. So now you had a dog whose testicles were removed before you left, because of a prostrate infection. There was some snide remarks, of course, as you did this to him, knowing about your own balls. As Italian brothers, this was a touchy subject. But you and Matt did a job on that poor dog. He was the hungriest dog anyone had ever seen, looking for meat in any movement of a human hand. His nose following conversational gestures like a conductors baton, sniffing, smelling, always hoping meat would appear in a palm, fall from a hand and into his mouth. But it never did. He went crazy instead. He lost his head. He began going around in circles. Three thousand dollars later, your brother called Australia, and gave you a progress report. He'd had acupuncture, chiropractric treatments, massage, many supplements. Matt was doing the responsible thing to bring Frankie out of his illness, but to no avail. Frankie, finally couldn't even get up. He developed paralysis and lay there near coma unable to eat one more vegetable with the supplements sprinkled on the top. And still he wouldn't die. Your mother and father and brother took him to the Humane Society where the vet gave him the needle. He was dead in a second. And everyone spilled their tears on that beautiful shepherd's coat. The coat that had been kept beautiful by twelve years of cortisone, to prevent coastal itch. The cortisone had destroyed certain functions of the organs, it turned out. That's what

8

cortisone does long term. And you knew it. Your brother knew it. But you let it go on. The Humane Society people were a fat young Mexican man and a fat older white woman with rouge and blue eyelids like a lizard, and mammoth tight jeans. They stood by as Frankie was mauled by your parents, handled with near animal paws themselves, as they cried and cried and said goodbye. A good buy was more like it. A hundred dollars to cremate Frankie, including the urn. The urn would be buried with you in just a mere month later. Little did your family know that they would be putting Frankie's ashes into your coffin soon. Your mother took a lock of Frankie's hair, like she would any grandchild.

BECAUSE YOU WANTED PLEASURE. Because you wanted that good feeling heroin gives you, you knew it was only a matter of time before you bought it, went back to your room and shot it into your vein, and planned to sit back and turn yourself over the the pleasure center of your brain. Your life was all set out in a picture before you with your family clustered into the apartment in Santa Barbara, Ralph in India, several broken hearted girlfriends licking their wounds here and there, and you were in a beautiful foreign country in an area where many Americans go to study Yoga. An "enlightened" crowd. Fun and interesting people. A tropical foliage all about, flowers, warmth, summer coming. Vacation spirit all around you. And your desire to enhance. Just give it a little boost. Even though your brother likes to think you took heroin to drown pain. He will have spent a fortune talking to your friends in the little suburb outside Sydney to see if they noticed any anguish in you, any discontent. And he finally got a bead on it from the Scotsman you passed out flyers for. He said, at the pub, when you came to join him, he could see a little upset in your eyes behind the joviality. That you had lots of women. That you were happy, except for that little furtiveness in your eyes, which Matt interpreted as worry over your life. But other friends at the funeral knew as your general restlessness for more. That you were never satisfied with reality once you knew you could have more than reality. When you can get that something extra from heroin.

ALL THE YOGA books in the world could not dissuade you from craving the shortcut to peace, joy, ecstasy, pure absence of life scraping on your nervous system. There was nothing to compare with that painkiller. All the Lotus positions, deep breathing, clearing the mind, exhaling the bad air, breaking through all the clogged places from the past that you supposedly hold in your musculature, could compete with heroin. It was only a matter of time. And no family love, mother's milk, father's drawing the line, setting boundaries, attempts to channel your energies and interests into the old work ethic by chastising and badgering to get a nine to five job like a normal human being and act like a man could save you from what you could get from heroin. Heroin combined with cocaine. And they get it from Korea over here. And it's four times stronger they told Matt later. But you didn't know that exactly. You'd heard stories, but you guessed at the dosage as you measured it out, melted it down, syringed it up, and looked for the bubble, and when all seemed just right, injected the needle into your vein. And you did have well-defined veins. Lean Italian arms with muscle and tendon from all the tension of holding Yoga positions and stretches. When your roommate downstairs heard the thump, as you fell forward dead, when your heart stopped and your head hit the floor, she thought you were doing your Yoga workout. That's what she told Matt when he called looking for answers. And after that, Matt knew that if only the paramedics could have been called you would have been saved. That knowledge would go to the grave with him.

MATT DRIVES, wondering what it could be that your mother could not tell him about you over the phone. She kept his beeper number just for something like this. For emergencies, when he was away from a phone. He always called her and gave her the motel number where he stayed, or called to check in regularly. His girlfriend, who knew nothing of your drug habit used to tease him about being a mama's baby. She would wonder why he called all the time. That no amount of time could pass without his checking in with his mother. It struck her as strange, but she passed it off as an Italian son's duty, since she was not Italian. She laughed at it in her pleasant times, and got irritated and ridiculed him when her mood changed. Still he kept your secret. The family secret that only you and your mother and father knew. Even after five and a half years she would be dumbfounded to have Matt reveal to her that you overdosed on cocaine and heroin. It would finally shut her mouth as she took in the story of how he had been obsessed with saving your life for twenty years. How he was always distracted and seemed preoccupied when they were together. Your brother with the priestly eyes. She would understand why he prayed and read the little Zen Buddhist handbook on daily thought to stay tranquil. She would reflect on her reckless attitude of making fun of his constant vigilance. About what? She used to shout, exasperated. But he refused to share your drug habit with her and break the trust you counted on not to tell anyone.

SO, THE DREADED CALL has come, at last, and she has dialed Matt's beeper. When it goes off, he takes the first off ramp and rings her. She simply says, in a grim voice, "Come home." It's like a thunderbolt to his heart. He knows the many voices of his mother and can detect a certain tragic note.

HE FIGHTS overwhelming anxiety. All the Buddha sayings books in the world can't buoy him up. He tries for all the ways he's trained himself to transcend the moment and find some serenity, but nothing works. He knows it's about you. He fears that you got back on drugs. He plans his strategy in dealing with you on the other side of the earth. He will insist on you coming home. And once home will renege on the ticket to India. But he will not let on when he speaks with you on the phone. He plans not to give you a ticket to India no matter what kind of a fuss or threat you cause. It's three thousand dollars, and the enrollment for yoga students is full at the Center near New Deli, with a three year waiting list. You had to have reservations in advance to even get on the waiting list in hope someone will not show up.

AND MATT DOESN'T WANT you to be away from your parents for a whole year. He is your keeper. He is his brother's keeper like no other. He's on his way home in his beloved rented car, a brand new Honda Acura with cruise control, heading south down the 101. He drives without his foot on the pedal. He believes that holding his foot on the gas pedal is a strain to be avoided. Why add to the stress to your life if there is such an invention as driving without touching the gas pedal. His feet are resting easy on the floor mat, slip-on penny loafers without the pennies, but with the tassels. Brown, shiny. Perfectly polished. He is that way. His attire is always creased by the iron in the right places, and in the course of a day, is never dirtied or wrinkled. In his closet in your parent's house hangs the same kind of slacks and shirts, all freshly done at his favorite Chinese laundry. He looks immaculate at all times. Except for his ever growing beard. He shaves every third day to protect his baby skin. That is the only sign of activity about your brother. The Sicilian beard pushing out of his fine Neapolitan skin. While you got the Neapolitan fine baby hair with hardly any beard. Like your mother's people.

MATT'S BEEN UP IN THE BAY AREA working. He's the good son who works, is steady, and stays and watches over the parents, lives without excesses, unless you can call having no excesses, excessive. He has no extravagances, no abundances. No emotions. He is the still and quiet one, who watches and acts when the family needs it. He does it all, so you don't have to do anything. He is the responsible son. You

13

get to be the one who can go play. It's always been that way. Let Matt handle all the business. You told him just recently over the phone that he was not happy unless he was controlling things. But who did you call when you needed money. And how did you get it out of him? If you were out of control and could worry him he'd always cough up what you needed. It's always worked. He didn't want you to die. To go on the street. He saved your life each time, he believed. He didn't know how to tell you no.

WHEN HIS BEEPER RANG, your mother simply said to come home. She does not tell him what it is. That's the way your family handles things. She doesn't want him to run off the road crying on the way home. So he runs through his mind what it could be. He knows it's about you. Perhaps you have come home early according to the talk the two of you had over the phone. He didn't want you to extend your stay another six months. He told you he'd give you a ticket to India if you'd come home on January 21, as planned, see Mommie and Daddy, as you both called your parents, even at 43 and 48. And after that you could go off to India to follow Ralph, the Yoga instructor you were studying under. He winces, remembering how he changed his mind after talking to Ralph. Ralph told him you had an attitude problem, that you'd learned all you could at the Center, and to go home. And for him not to give you any money. To make you stand on your own two feet.

"GO HOME," HE SAID, "go teach what you've learned here in Sydney, back in America. Go teach your students back in Santa Barbara." But that didn't sit well with you, Billy. Your brother, good old Matti, who'd always bailed you out, offered the ticket to India to follow Ralph, and then he took it away and said to come home and you'd discuss plans to go to India. It all rang suspicious to you. He also said you owed the money you borrowed to go to Australia. That seven hundred dollar round trip ticket. That your Workman's Compensation check had come in, and the family was going to deduct what they lent you. And your voice fell. You said, "Really?" in disbelief that they expected you to pay your own way. That they were going to keep your money to pay themselves back. That family of yours, sitting there with plenty, and not letting you have a free ride. You knew that tone of voice would tear at your brother's heart strings. He feared your addiction. He feared disappointing you. He feared that you should have a sad or mad feeling. He feared giving and not giving to you. He didn't know which way you'd go. To give or not to give? That became the big question. And he had always come through out of fear you'd go to strangers and get killed doing drugs.

BUT NOW, YOUR TEACHER, Ralph, spoke up. And he listened. It would be a decision Matt would regret for the rest of his life. He would question his motives. Three thousand dollars for the ticket. And after the funeral your family would be cursing the simple three thousand dollars up against the ten thousand it cost to have your body shipped back, treated in the mortuary over there and again over here, plus international fees here and there. It was an immediate four thousand dollars just like that. No questions asked. The Consulate called, sent a letter of condolences and business and the amount to handle it in a case like this. Your brother and your father went to the bank and withdrew the money and sent it the next day. And just as simple, after a phone call to the funeral parlor here, the next lump sum was given, and again your family went to the bank. Matt kept asking, wondering, pondering, chastising himself over feeling that bit of relief that he did not have to spend three thousand on the India ticket, as people are wont to do, even rich people, when they "get out of" some expense. And that relief festered into superstition. "If I had just sent the ticket...." And he'd cry, thinking he could have saved your life. Just one more time. Just one more need. Just one more rescue. Just one more giving you what it was you wanted. Maybe that would have turned your life around and you would have gotten off drugs. Just the India experience. Maybe there would have been something said there that would have clicked inside your head to make you kick the cocaine and heroine habit. This would be your brother's dilemma. He would never know, even though people would try to hammer it home that you had already done this in the past and it hadn't helped. That he had already saved your life by twenty years. That's what all your party buddies who showed up said. They thought you wouldn't live past twenty the way you were "partying' at fifteen, shooting up, wanting to get a little bit higher than everyone else.

DID RALPH'S REJECTION of you, sending you home, hurt? That was another theory Matt had. Perhaps it dampened your ego. Oh, poor baby, in your big brother's mind. He believed in your frailty. And Ralph not knowing how sensitive you were. And, as a teacher only four years older, ordering you out of his country, out of his territory, out of the Center For Yoga. You told your big brother on him, though. You said he was irritable and nasty to you at times and you never knew why. You said he acted like a....(asshole) and wondered what was eating him. He had everything you wanted, a Yoga school, prestige, the ability to tie his body in a knot and bring in an audience. You said that he was the one with the attitude. That he sat and taught yoga, the deep breathing, inner peace, and then drank forty cups of coffee a day, and yelled at you and bossed you around, and argued over money and taking his students away from him. That he forbade you to teach yoga in your rented room in that big house where they found you. That until you "got yourself together," you were not to teach yoga on your own, only in affiliation with him as his assistant. And that he was leaving for India and wanted you to go home in his absence. There was the talk you had, that at some future point, you would be his assistant yoga instructor as he traveled through Europe. But he never brought the subject up again.

THERE'S YOUR BROTHER, parking his car in the stall under the car port of your parents' apartment building. He makes his way up the steps and knocks on the door. They keep their door locked at all times. They are from New York, and even after fifteen years in California, still think it is unsafe to leave your door unlocked during the day. Your brother has a key, but as he's getting it out, your mother comes to the door with a look on her face that makes your brother's heart fall. He can see that she is afraid and collapses against his chest, groaning the worst words she will ever have to say in her life. "Billy is dead." And then, in a strangely hopeless and empty voice which will stay with her for a long time, she adds, "You'd better call them. Here's the number. The Consulate." The words come with such difficulty that your brother pushes her back and holds her so he can see her face, watch her mouth, and lip read. He shouts, "Noooooo," like an opera singer, and switches to a barely audible hiss, "this can't be." The neighbors on either side can hear if they're home. People walking by can hear, if they're walking by. It is a cry your brother will make many times before he has taken in this information that he does not want to accept.

THERE THEY ARE. YOUR FAMILY. Your father turning to your brother, but wanting to handle it himself, and gruffing around. He's the man, after all. The father. He is suppose to take charge. But he gives way to Matt. He is helpless to pursue the Consulate on his own, although he takes it and tries to grab the paper out of your brother's hand. Your mother elbows him aside, and turns her back on your father and looks only to her first son to find out if this is true or not. She has always turned to Matt. Matt has always been her little man. She does not like her husband much. He has yelled at her for too many years. She finds no solace in his company. Their relationship gives them no comfort. They have been at each other's throats for over fifty years, and now this. He gives her a long hard blue-eyed look, trying to read how she is going to take this news, now that she can let go in the safety of her first son. He is afraid the grief will replace his hold on her and she will develop an autonomy outside him. He has been able to control her all these years, and now she will have feelings that are out of his reach. She keeps her face averted from his and faces only Matt with the look of a trusting school girl. Matt will know what to do. Your father is left standing there outside their duo. He is the odd one out. He cannot penetrate what the mother and first son have together. A definite bonding that does not include him. He hikes around the carpeted livingroom like he's on a hillside, eyeing them. He clamps his mouth shut, chewing on his false teeth, and shakes his head, his baby blue eyes focused on those two, as Matt dials the American Consulate in Sydney, Australia.

IT IS CONFIRMED. No one can sit down, even though Matt tries to place his mother in a chair. She won't bend. She can't be still. They pace and face each other. You are dead. Billy is dead. It rhymes. They don't notice. They don't care. There is no humor. There never will be. Matt looks at his father to see if it registers just what all his yelling has finally caused to happen. He sees the father glower back, daring him to blame him for this. He bites down hard on his dentures, so that his lips and cheeks bulge like Popeye. All he lacks is a pipe. The mother watches Matt, and then looks down and whimpers to her own chest. Matt comes to her aid, wrapping his arms around her shoulders and cradling her, holding tight, as if he can protect her from this. As if it is on the outside, and he can use his own body as armor. So, there they are, as you lie dead in a mortuary in the outskirts of Sidney, Australia.

MATT FINDS OUT all the detail he can in the next few hours. First he calls his girlfriend. He screams the words to her over the phone. Billy is dead. He died in Australia from an overdose. They found him in his room with a needle by his arm. Little by little the story will be pieced together. There is a mixture of curiosity and disbelief in the apartment when Matt's girlfriend arrives. She comes in, taller than the family, awkward. It is not her family, and she has a sharp tongue, as Matt knows, out of the earshot of the mother and father. She acts polite, like company, while around them. Matt calls her for her support, but when he sees her face, he searches for something he never finds there. She understands, but does she really care. He knows she has a family of her own, and that is where her feelings are. She will come over and be there with them, but sit on the couch, and still act like a visitor, not family. He is glad she has come. It is the first of the many audiences he will orchestrate, so that his parents can demonstrate their prostration. He tells her that his cousins Hugh and Lydia will be here soon. She is relieved. Lydia is the perfect sayer of things. She says what people are suppose to say at a time like this. She will never shed a tear, but hold strong, as she believes through her Catholic training to do. She converted when she married Hugh. Hugh is the contractor with the youthful manner. They have just come from a vacation in Mexico and their faces are rosy with sunshine. Their clothes are bright cottons and denim. They are a couple that still look like dolls on the wedding cake even thirty years after the marriage. She aged with bright white hair that brings out her clear blue eyes. She keeps a smile on her lips which is the socially acceptable face she wears at work in her personnel job. Her wardrobe is always brand new red, white, and blue patriotic colors and styles. The sailor collars and skirts just below the knee, or the slick pants suits with heels. They come in looking brand new and absolutely clean and fresh. At fifty-five, they may as well be twenty-five for their attitude toward life and simple living. Lydia goes immediately to your mother and holds her in a guarded, careful hug. She pats her, as if the grief manual told her to do so. And Hugh stands back and lets his wife perform the rituals. Almost as if she's a ventriloquist, the right words begin to enter the room, float through the air and comfort the grieving ones. Matt begins a speech of self-chastisement that Lydia tries to talk him out of. And once, heard, lets silence fall, and then curses,

"You stupid bastard, Billy." He curses you and holds his fist is punch position, that makes it known that if you were here, he would kill you for doing this to yourself so that he and your parents have to suffer.

INTERMITTENTLY, as Lydia and Hugh dazzle the small apartment with their flash and flair for staying brand new in spite of everything, the male members of your family will say that they cannot believe this is happening. They will think of new people to call to confirm it. They will repeat what each person tells them many times. They will curse and then cry. Your mother is the only one who won't curse you. She will begin to notice all the reminders you left behind and fear them. She will point out the picture of the sunset in a frame on the wall that you took. She will point to the inlay of a dog you made at school, and framed on another wall. Her voice will come as a groan as she lists to Lydia that you left all of your books in the bookshelf, and all your clothes in the closet, and your guitar under the bed. The smile will never leave Lydia's lips as she nods and agrees that they are there, and that you did, indeed, exist and left them behind. Your mother will listen and make no response. She will be beyond reaching. She will listen to Lydia's perfunctory statements of comfort, and just sit there in the recliner, stunned, groaning with the grief every once in awhile. Hugh will stand back as if he's at a basketball game and stare out of his dark eyes, taking it all in, unable to participate.

YOUR GIRLFRIEND will stay over. You want her to. She will sleep in one of the twin beds, side by side. The same beds you sweated out your withdrawals in for the three months you lived with your parents after being evicted, before going to Australia. Two narrow beds where your father and brother sleep. Your mother has her own room and her own double-sized bed. Your parents haven't slept together for years. Matt doesn't remember how many it's been. It doesn't matter to him. He doesn't know if your parents have a sex life or not. He can't conceive of such a thing and doesn't want to know. These are questions his girlfriend asks him, which he doesn't answer. He simply shows her where she will sleep, silent, struck by learning of your death. It's been only a matter of six hours since receiving the call from the Consulate. So new is your death, that their minds are still in a state of adjustment, trying to take it in. The expected tears don't flow as your family thinks they should. Your family has a lot of 'spose tos and shoulds. They are a traditional family from Long Island. Your brother calls your family, "ethnic, blue collar Italians." On the East Coast death has a certain definite response from a family. You make calls, you tell relatives. They pass the word. Calls begin to come in. You wait for certain people you know know about the death. With each call you cry all over again, just telling it. The phone should keep ringing. You tell it into the night. You finally sit down, the three family members left, and feel one another's presence. That's all there is. And someone says how many calls there were. If it is a large number of calls, there is some comfort in that. If not that many people paid their respects by phone, you mention that. You expect to share the death with as many people as possible. It is not the California way, though. In fact, some relatives born out here, younger members of the family clan, remain silent, giving you privacy at this personal time.

YOUR PARENTS DON'T UNDERSTAND this, though. It hurts them. They remember the funerals from their own childhoods where family members would not think of remaining silent. They shake their heads over the trend in death announcements out here.

EACH CALLER TOLD how good you were, Billy. What a guy. Well, what else would they say. And when they heard you were a heroin addict, they still sympathized through their curiosity, managing to get out a few questions of, "How long has he done this? Why didn't you ever tell us. We could have helped you bear up under it all these years. Why did you keep it to yourself?" A mild chastisement while giving condolences.

AND SO THE EVENING GOES. Matt's face strikes the mask of tragedy ever so often, in a primal scream open-mouthed anguish. His face is wet. He swings his fist at the air. The invisible foe was always there, but he could never punch him down. And now he got you. He goes from saying, "shit, this is unreal, you stupid idiot," to "I can't believe this is happening. Why did you do it." To, "This is sad." A simple understatement he repeats dozens of times during the evening. Your father keeps his head bent, chin on his chest, face red, hair white, eyes blue. A real patriot, like Lydia, his niece by marriage. He takes out his teeth and grinds his gums and the choking sounds come intermittently. It is not an easy sound. The anguish gets caught in his throat and he has to bark it through. He has just spent tears on your dog, Frankie. Now those tears look like folly. Tears for a dog, when now it's you. He sounds like he's strangling.

HE TELLS MATT'S GIRLFRIEND that he's been in WWII, and has seen bodies blow up all around him. He knows about death. But he is worried about Jewell. He nods toward his wife who sits alone. She has not turned to him for comfort at all. He has not come to her and put his arm around her. She has not lain her head on his chest. He has not looked into her eyes to try to find a meeting of the mind. The evening is long and the night is longer. No one gets any sleep. Everyone goes through the ritual. Your father first, goes into the bathroom and does what he does before bed, then turns on the little T.V. in your mother's room. He will sleep with her tonight so Matt's girlfriend can have the twin bed beside Matt. Then your mother goes in and brushes her teeth and wipes down her face with moisturizer. She puts on her nightgown and slippers and a robe and comes out again. She wants to sit in front of the television in the livingroom and keep anything on to distract her. She is afraid of the dark, of the night, of the long hours where she will be lying there knowing you are in a box on the other side of the earth. She has said so. "He's in a box over there. How can I sleep?" And she must sleep next to your dad. It is a repugnant idea. They will not touch. If he does try to reach over with a rough paw to pat her, she will brush him away, the way she does anywhere.

YOUR BROTHER'S GIRLFRIEND is tired. She is a stranger to the family even after five years. She regards it as a family outside and away from herself. Just Matt's family. She does not feel close to anyone, nor does she want to. She goes to bed wearing one of Matt's shirts and nothing else. Sometime in the wee hours your mother will see her stark naked, making her way to the bathroom. Matt goes to bed, but not until his mother does. He sits with her until she is nodding off. He cups her face in his hands and studies it. He believes she is too frail to take your death. He will keep an ear cocked toward her room all night and rush to her if there is any sound. He knows his father will be of no use. And so the lights are turned off, except for a night light, the street lights coming in through the blinds, and the bathroom light left on with the door ajar. There are the sounds of passing traffic off in the distance once in awhile, and then nothing.

MORNING COMES as grim as a morning can be. Your mother simply pads from her bed to her chair in the livingroom and sits there and cries. Your brother goes to her and tends her with pettings about the head and shoulders, and then walks silently into the kitchen nook and makes her a supplemental drink of all the ingredients she will need to help relieve grief. He has read the supplement manual, and has lists of what is good for what. It is his profession, after all. He puts the drink on a coaster on the table beside her chair and she sips at it. Eme, your girlfriend gets up after trying to sleep hard and late, so not to have to face all this, and showers, dresses, and suggests everyone go out for breakfast. It is met with silent poker faces. If you can't go out with us, then no one will go out. Your father has already gone out. He gets up earlier than anyone and dons his sneakers and sweats and is off to swim at the gym, and then will arrive home in an hour or so for breakfast. So Eme runs out and brings breakfast back from the nearby health restaurant. Potatoes, muffins, coffee, buckwheat pancakes.

YOUR MOTHER PICKS. Your father is ravenous. And your brother eats with some gusto, too. And then what is there to do. With eating a necessity, the morning was used up ever so slowly, and now there is the rest of the day to spend. And the rest of their lives. Without you. They are a bedraggled trio. They keep busy on the telephone to Sydney. They want to find out all they can. And the business of shipping you home (they never say "your body") is utmost on their minds. They want you here with them. Cost is of no importance anymore. Whatever it takes. The phone bill, too. It doesn't matter anymore, when, before, they would count the minutes and try not to talk too long to you. After all, they earned their money the hard way, and their habits are still intact.

MATT CALLS THE CONSTABLE. He was the one the roommate called to report your death. He has all the details. You find that he will be mailing them to you after the coroner fills out all the papers. it will take awhile. Maybe weeks. Your family will have to wait to find out what you shot into your arm that killed you. There will be an autopsy and a report made. You mother is stabbed by any word concerning your body. You. She clutches herself and huddles against her own body, curled forward, as if cradling a baby. And she sits all day. Her life has stopped now that yours has. She does not go into the kitchen. She does not clean house. She does not shop. She does nothing but sit and listen to your brother finding out what to do about your death. And she puts the television on to watch the flood, the O.J. Simpson trial, anything. She tries to read the paper. She doesn't go for a walk. She doesn't go to the club where her lady friends will seek her out to give their condolences. She rocks herself in her chaise lounge chair afraid of your death, and sometimes bites her thumbnail. You know this gesture of hers. Like a little child. A lost child. One who doesn't know what to do in the world.

THE TOWELS MUST BE LAUNDERED. They've been used their allotted time of the week and now Matt makes them into a bundle of laundry. There are a few other things to fill up the load for the machine in the laundry room across the grounds over there. And now your mother must pull against gravity and lift herself from the chair and gather up the laundry. You know how your family is over things like this. it is a ritual that takes much thinking and fussing and seems to be almost an impossibility at a time like this. Even before your death, laundry day was an ordeal all of you got through and felt better when it was over. You mother painstakingly goes through the house and picks up whites. Anything white and light that will fit with the towels. And Matt waits. He is impatient with this duty, wanting to get it done and overwith so that he and your mother can go back to mourning undisturbed again. He follows your mother and takes any garment from her hand as soon as she picks it up, and tucks it into the bundle he holds. At last the agony of hunting for dirty clothes and passing by your clothes all hanging there in the upper closet, never to be worn by you again, is over. Your mother whimpered through the whole task, and is exhausted as she sits back down in her chair. Matt pats her old cheeks and is off down the stairs and across the walkway to the laundry room, with the key. You mother simply sits now, with her head bowed. She closes her eyes and waits. She groans a little. It hurts so bad that you are not coming home. She pictures you dead. And so the second morning goes.

MATT'S GIRLFRIEND SUGGESTS you all go out for breakfast again. Yesterday she went out and brought it back. Now, today, it's a beautiful sunny day. It would be good to walk over to The Good Earth and have a nice hearty serving of potatoes and eggs, wheat flour pancakes, coffee. Matt, who has returned, says we have to wait for the laundry and wait for your father to come back from the gym. Eme is impatient. After the laundry commotion and strain, she wants to get out of the apartment. It shouldn't have caused such a stress just to do the laundry. She takes Matt outside on the stairs and sits in the sun and tells him this. She says she is becoming you. She is vehement under the strain of being around your family, and must hiss in his ear like a snake. She says she now knows why you had to go out and try to find something away from your family. That the family is deadly. It is no fun. It is all ritualizing chores and such. That it is driving her crazy and she must have more. She must walk. Be outdoors. That her family always threw open all the doors and windows in the morning and met the day. That her mother sang opera hanging out the laundry. That there was definite joy for no reason at all except that they carried it inside themselves and it simply came out when everyone woke up. And now, his family is like death. The apartment is like a morgue. She rants in a near whisper so your mother won't hear. She is a different kind of creature who finds herself trapped with a family that she can't approve of. Matt stands there and hears her out, but doesn't waver from his position. He knows his family. He can't imagine things being any other way. He allows for her response to it, knowing how she is with her own family. A California outdoors type of people. Hearty and expressive and demonstrative. And slightly messy. They live the way he couldn't possibly live.

AND SO, THE SPAT IS OVER, and Eme sits and waits at the bottom of the stairway in the sunshine, and finally after a long while, after your father has come home from his swim at the gym, and the laundry

30

is done, and your mother has taken off her duster and put on some slacks and a sweatshirt, and Eme has offered to go pick up the laundry and bring it back so everyone can get ready, everyone comes down the stairs and walks to The Good Earth.

NOW ANOTHER RITUAL BEGINS. Your father knows the owner. He likes to bring him over to the table and motion for the tall old guy to bend down right near your father's mouth with his ears. It must be a New Yorker's way to get buddy-buddy with the boss. And so it goes. Your father takes the owner aside this time, as soon as he enters, and tells him about his son dying in Australia. He leans into the tall man's chest and gets a clap on the shoulders as he breaks down against the man ever so briefly, and then, as quickly as it starts, it ends. Man to man, it is. You have only to give a hint of your emotions, not go on until they're messy. And no one in your family can say the actual words without their voices breaking. They do not want to say them. Saying them makes them too true.

AT THE BOOTH, your mother and father fuss over what they will have. Matt orders all side dishes for his health. It is a glum breakfast. Your mother barely picks at her potatoes. Your father wolfs down the pancakes because he is hungry from his swim and determined that your death will not take him down. He is angry with you. He keeps shaking his head in disbelief and anger. He keeps eyeing his wife and living son for any sign that they blame him. All he ever wanted to do was to shape you up. He didn't understand why

31

you wouldn't work like everyone else. Like he did. At fourteen, his hard-working father sent him out on the streets of New York to deliver papers, collect milk bottles, and do anything else to make money. He worked every day of his life from that age on. And when you came along he tried to raise you right. He never understood what went wrong. You started doing Yoga. He never wants to hear that word again he's told us. That wasn't a real job. He has such a look of disgust on his face over your life style that your mother just sniffles to herself, helpless, disliking your father for disapproving of your interests.

YOUR MOTHER PASSES her leftovers to Matt, who gobbles them down. Your father passes his to Matt, who eats them, too. Matt seems famished. Unless food is put right in front of him, he doesn't eat. He has lost weight in the two days since hearing about your death. Your mother has not cooked, and doesn't seem to intend to resume her duties. When everyone gets home, your father expects her to go about them, and be who she was before your death. She simply sits down in her chair and doesn't budge. She ignores him completely. Matt pampers her, opening the sliding glass door ever so much to circulate fresh air into the apartment, closing the front door to give privacy. The phone begins to ring. It rings and rings all day. It will ring for the next ten days without more than ten minutes in between people calling. Matt will grab it and talk for an hour at a time, crying in that primal agony at first and then settling into giving information about your death. He has two voices. It is all your friends from the East Coast. Men who grew up with you, who used to shoot up with you, but finally gave it up, got married, bought homes, had children. They all try to get Matt to stop blaming himself. They all remember how you liked to party. They all kind of smile over the miles, so that your can hear the smile come through the telephone receiver over your intention of never getting a nine-to-five and settling down. They all said you died happy. They all tell Matt that there was nothing he could have done to stop the inevitable. That he did what he said he wanted to do, save you. That he saved you all these years. That he did rescue you.

EVERYONE HAS A REASON for your death. One old relative says the only way Matt could have prevented your death was four walls and a key. He makes the gestures. Others hold to the belief that your time was up. That when you get called there's nothing anyone can do. That, it's just meant to be. Your old girlfriends believe down deep that it was over them. They take the credit or the blame, depending on their level of love for you. You left several broken hearts it turns out. At least three. These women are devastated by the news, but in a different way than your family. They simply can't believe it. But they have lives that buoy them up. They call and talk to your mother and tell her how much they loved you and how sorry they are that you are dead. Your mother doesn't think much of their lamentings. It is all noise in her ear at this point. if these women who loved you so much, did, in fact, love you that much, then what happened. Why did you never marry one, have babies, set up a life. She puts down the phone with fatigue. It tires her, to hear about their love now. It's too late. She doesn't even want to know about your chances at happiness and a full life. And, besides, she already knows. She knew about each one as it happened. There was this one and that one you brought to the house. And then the other one. She met them all. The main ones. Then there were rumors of others she never met, because they didn't amount to anything. You pursued women. You couldn't go too long without one. One friend will tell that you could pick up a woman in five minutes after entering a room, while it took the rest of them an hour. There was something about you. The smile, the humor, the good Italian lover boy looks. Your style. Your clothes. They had to be cut just right to show off your Yoga body. The slenderness, the muscles, the proportions. You were proud of yourself. You had your hair styled just so by your mother's hairdresser. You saw to every detail of your grooming. All the products that your brother bought for you that were environmentally safe and animal-cruelty-free. You had it made, man. Made in the shade. You were a rascal. A good-looking, good-for-nothing son of a bitch, by some people's standards.

MATT HAS GATHERED information. The phone bill to Sydney will be astronomical. He doesn't care anymore. Only your father tries to get him to stop lying on his back with his eyes closed talking and talking to the other side of the world. The phone planted, almost permanently against that side of his head. Every time your father looks, there's Matt talking to New York or Australia or to relatives and friends in this town. Yammering and yammering. Telling and retelling in his almost inaudible monotone. You father has no patience with people talking on the phone for hours as if there is nothing else to do in life. Even before your death, he had a thing about Matt and the phone. And now, there will be no end to the hours of talking over it, and the bill. In his day, people didn't run up phone bills. It was considered decadent. Only rich people did that, he supposed, but not the hard-working working class. You didn't stay on the phone. You wrote letters. Or you visited each other. This phone business was a sore point with him. Yet, your brother lies there all day long, as if floating on a magic carpet, and talks and talks to anyone and everyone, so that when he finally sits up right, and pads around the house, he seems in a trance. When he finally rests the receiver in the cradle by the kitchen nook, he is dazed with being back. As long as he keeps talking and telling it and listening to people try to take it away from him, he is okay. When he hangs up, reality sets in and his eyes are half mast and watery, trying not to see the truth.

ON THE THIRD DAY, the Constable promises to send the report. And the American Consulate in Sydney promise to take care of business. They will ship you back to Los Angeles. The mortuary there will arrange it so that the mortuary here will meet the plane and pick you up. it will cost more than any ticket could possibly cost alive. Dead, you are much more expensive to handle. They will have to refrigerate you. Keeping your live body warm is cheaper for an airline, of course. Feeding a live body is cheaper, of course. When you flew over you sat upright and took up less space. You were one of many passengers. Now, you fly alone, prone. It is more trouble. There are certain people hired to handle you. The box you are in is heavy. it requires a special hoist, a special car. The whole picture changes. The whole attitude of the employees for the airline changes. Transportation becomes a problem. There are so many factors to consider. But they have it all figured out. They must take much more care with you, not to damage you, than when you were alive. Alive, you could take your chances. Your mother should have worried then. Dead, they dare not destroy a hair on your head, or mess you up in any way. Dead, you are precious cargo. You are worth four thousand dollars. Over, you were worth seven hundred. Remember the bargain you got, calling that ticket outlet. Round trip only seven hundred. Little did you know that your property in Colorado would be sold to pay for your transportation back. To pay back the family's bank account. Four thousand to the Consulate, another four thousand to the Home, as they call it, here. Plus extras. The funeral home calls your brother and wonders if the casket he ordered over the phone will be right. It's an octagonal shape. Like in the horror movies. The rounded upper portion, and the long lower portion. It looks like a monster's box. The kind Boris Karloff would wake up in with a stiff rigor mortis back and limbs and stomp around scaring people from. Your brother takes the phone into the bedroom, so not to alarm your mother. He orders a nice squared-off casket. A pretty grey-silver one. And they want the clothes. The body will arrive on Thursday. At that time they will need to dress you.

YOUR BROTHER COMES OUT of the bedroom stricken. The thought of that conversation wrecking his face. The primal scream there in silence. He puts on a poker face for your mother, as if the call was about nothing at all. You mother looks up at Matt's face, searching for meaning. And in a distant voice, somewhere far away, she asks, "Who was that?" She really doesn't want to know, and counts on Matt to protect her. He will tell her what she wants to hear. He brushes it aside now, and says, just the Home, nothing really. That word kills her. It's as if she's been stabbed. You will not be coming home. You will be shipped to that place. It is too much: She goes over into herself, rounded down to a nub, sobbing, choking like your dad. Dying now, herself.

THE PHONE RINGS ALL THE TIME, and your brother gets it, while your mother watches the O.J. Simpson trial to try to distract herself. She was going to tell you all about it. Now she watches it in a whole new light. All that she sees happening, you will never know. During her watching, it occurs to her over and over again that you will never know the outcome of the trial. She whimpers intermittently all day. Your father strides through the house in disapproval. He bats at the trial with his seventy-nine year old paw. He shakes his head back and forth. A deep frown about the mouth and an implied scoff. He insists your mother finally get up and begin preparing the evening meal. He will not allow her to indulge herself any more. He's had it with the two of them, hugging each other, bawling out loud, sitting around inactive. Never getting out of their pajamas. He goes off into the bedroom to rest after his workout. Later he will come out and prepare hors d'oeuvres of salsa, chips and guacamole and pour himself and your mother a glass of wine. He, red, her, white. He will try to ignore the whole subject of your death. He is already tired of it.

YOUR FATHER IS A SOLVER of problems and this one cannot be solved. He is the "head of the family" and believes his position implies control and leadership. And now your death is something too big to take on. He is dwarfed by it, made too small for the big job ahead. He tries to pretend it's not there, and this way he can get up in the morning and go out and continue with the routine that he's done for years for his own survival. He's a tough man on the outside, and careful of his tender lining. He must act like a man and not cave in, in front of your mother. Only at crucial times, just before going to bed, or over a phone call from his elderly sister, does he bawl like a calf, and then choke it off with, "Ok, ok." He puts a stop to his tears with those words. As if saying, "Enough, already." He is a man who is afraid of excessive behavior. He is deathly afraid of emotion. People expressing their feelings makes him turn away and give them their privacy. He has spent his life being moderate, careful, meticulous in daily habits. He lives small and close and with caution. He will not drive at night. He will not take chances. He takes his car for check-ups regularly, so that driving it will be as safe as it can be mechanically. He tends to his person with utmost awareness, making sure he is alright all the time. That he is doing the right thing to keep up his health at almost eighty. He takes all the supplements Matt gives him. He grooms himself and exercises, and eats vegetarian. The only violation of himself is with the glass or two of wine at dinner, and occassionally a cup of real coffee at a cafe. Otherwise he listens to his son, Matt, the professional health scientist, who instructs him on healthful living. And then he gets the news that you are dead. It is too much. It comes like a bomb in the middle of his well-structured life, and perfectly ordered days. It interferes in the way he wants to feel. He was going along just fine, feeling good, except for his arthritis caused by getting his kneecap shot off in World War II; but, taking his cortisone for that, staying out of pain, taking each day at a time, and getting through it as best he could at his age, and then the Consulate called. And then the Constable gave their report. And then the Coroner was contacted. And each office dug deeper into his tranquility. Each official set off a chain reaction of thoughts and feelings that he had been avoiding all his life. He had had to bury his mother, his father, one sister. And now this. He trudges around the small apartment, shaking his shaggy, curly white hair, saying, "I never would have thought this could happen to my family. I never would have thought it." And goes off to watch his programs on the little black-and-white T.V. in the bedroom where he can try to laugh anyway. He likes those funny sitcoms. Any corny dialogue between a cast of bluecollar characters. He likes the blunt straight talk, the striking to the point, without finesse. He likes truth, and none of this beating around the bush. But, he does not like this truth. Your death. It will keep him from being able to laugh at Roseanne. It enrages him that you would do this to him. And intentionally. Not even accidentally. And to your mother and brother, who are less able to take it than he is. He hurts for them. They hurt for him. Everyone is afraid the other can't take it. And he, the "man" of the family must try to protect them all. Behind each other's backs they all tell one another, "Watch Matti, he's going to take it too hard. I'm afraid he won't make it." Or, "Keep an eye on your mother, I'm worried about her." Or, "Your dad may not get through this. He puts on an act, but underneath, he's worse off, in some ways, than we are. He has a lot of guilt. The way he treated Billy." And on and on, the family goes. Around and around like a merry-go-round, unable to say it aloud to each other's faces.

AND, THERE YOU ARE IN A BOX, missing out on all their grief. How would you grieve if you were in their place? They were worried about the way you wouldn't be able to handle your dog's death. The long phone calls. All the tears. Just the month before. In fact, they all wonder if it was grieving for your dog that sent you over the edge so that you sought relief in heroin again. That Frankie's death caused you to relapse. Matt is sure that was one factor. You were too far away for the family to watch you when you got the bad news. They offered to fly you home to be near you to help you through it. But you simply said, "What could I do? The dog is dead. Why come home?" Eme thought that was "realistic." She told Matt, "See, your brother's the only sensible one. He can take his dog's death in stride. It's only a dog, after all. If it meant more to him, he'd come home." But, what did she know. Matt never told her you were a heroin addict. No one knew until your death. And then something had to be said. Everyone asked how you died. All the relatives had to be told. All the friends. And everyone was surprised, at first, and then understood your family better. They had been sitting on this secret for years. Even your mother's sister, the one she goes to lunch every week with, didn't know. Your mother didn't want anyone to think of you that way. She hoped you'd get over it and she'd not have to have it as a secret. That there would be nothing to keep from anyone. That when she talked about you to her sister, it would be simply chit chat, and not this terrible harboring of the family secret. The lying by omission. Her sister felt betrayed when she found out. She would never look at her sister in the same way again now that she knew the amount of deceit she was capable of. All those years and all those lunches downtown, fifty-two times a year for the last fifteen years, and all those social gatherings, and telephone conversations. Nothing about her worries about Billy, the drug addict.

YOUR BODY ARRIVES in LAX on Thursday. Your parent's house is filled with bouquets of flowers people have sent. Your father has put them all out on the deck outside, out of sight. He hates flowers, ever since his mother's death. Your mother fights to keep a few of the most beautiful bouquets indoors on the dinning room table and sideboard. There is a huge fruit basket that Norma, the neighbor lady made up and brought over. Your Aunt Isabel has brought over food. There is a stack of cards your family has received. Your mother counts them. She counts the bouquets. She cries and cries, dipping her chin and making those helpless sounds. Sounds like no others she has ever made. She has never been so out of control, so that the sounds come, as with any animal in pain. They seep from her throat, an expression of her heart, and are beyond etiquette. She is almost embarrassed, letting go like this in front of people. She, the most self-possessed of all. It was your father who was the embarrassment, saying anything on his mind. Behaving like an unpolished laborer by her standards. Your mother was the one who kept the impeccably good manners, and now she is wet and weepy, nose running, eyes like black holes, mouth unrouged, hair just there with no thought about it, and this continuous sounds emitting on its own like a whipped dog tethered in the cold on a porch. She is made sloppy by your death. There is no way she can maintain her footing. The messiness of her beloved son's death is all over her.

WHILE THEY WAIT for Thursday, your mother apologizes that she is going to go have her hair done. She wonders what people will think. Eme encourages her. She whispers to Matt that why should she apologize. Does she think people will think she doesn't care about you lying cold in a casket, while she waltzes down to her Okinawan hairdresser? How could she think that. Does she surprise herself that she is capable of thinking of her hair while you lie dead? That she should violate the holiness of your death with thoughts of grooming and how she looks.

42

Matt just ignores Eme. These are questions no one in your family ever care to ask. Things are just what they are and no one is "rude" enough to probe. It is a kind of vulgar mind that must seek out motives. Motives should remain unexamined. There is a certain dignity in "just being." Matt has read all the Zen and Buddhist manuals for living. You just are. You don't have to know why everything happens. it shows lack of trust. And smacks of gossip and smut. He doesn't even want to think about his mother going to the hairdresser, and apologizing for it. All he does is hug her and pet at her shoulders and sorry loose cheeks, and kisses her head, the very hair that lies flat, and tells her it's okay, not to worry about it. He knows she likes her hair to stand up. She doesn't like it flat like this. And she needs color. She is thinking of being seen by everyone at the funeral. She doesn't want to look all grown out gray with the cinnamon tinge to the ends. Or for her hair to have grown out so that it hangs. She likes it out two to three inches long and held up away from her head and all warm brown. Eme tells her a shampoo and all that tender loving care will do her good. That, of course, she should go and know that it is a good thing to want to have her hair done. It falls on deaf ears. Eme is a California woman. There is no protocol in her life. Anything is okay with her. Whatever makes you feel good, do it. So, she mainly ignores anything she says. Eme's own children need more from her that they get. Not like mothers back in her day back east where people did certain things that their parents had done, and their parents before them. What does Eme know.

BUT YOUR MOTHER GOES and comes back looking the way she likes to look in spite of you dying, and reports in a groaning baritone barely audible that the hairdresser cried and wouldn't let her pay for the session. And then your mother takes to her chair and resumes her mourning.

THAT EVENING your mother begin to fret about the obituary. The funeral parlor says it is included in the price and they want it as soon as possible. The body will be here and the announcement in the paper is imperative if they want people to come to the funeral. And so, diligently, your mother begins to read other obituaries. Eme is visiting and sits by, putting in some suggestions. She's suppose to be a writer. Your mother tums to her for some advice, and she suggests the obvious, the brief listing of your personal history and current status just before death. Your mother reaches into the chairside table and finds a tablet in the little drawer. There is a pencil with it. She begins. You were born in Long Island, graduated from UCLA in Environmental Science, after attending your first two years at NYU and Syracuse University. She becomes impressed, as she jots this down. Thinking of all your education. She gestures toward all your books again. A whole bookcase full in her bedroom. All Matt's in the other bookcase in the other bedroom. This, from a mother who finished high school and then worked and met your father who didn't go to high school. He had an eighth-grade education and then went to work. She begins to tell little stories in contrast to your educational history. She and your father went to the same grammar school. That's where they met. They were childhood sweethearts. They fell in love as teenagers. Your father fell in love with your mother even before she was "developed." One of his Irish friends teased him about that. She was just a little girl, ha, ha, ha. And then your mother concentrates on your current status just before you died. You were at a sabbatical in Sydney, studying and teaching Yoga under the world-renowned Yoga master Ralph, at the Center for Yoga in Paddington. It all sounds important. In fact, it is true. What is left out is what you were really doing over there after the classes. That was an unknown element until this. Now, she wonders. How long had you been on heroin again. You had been clean for three years, and then obviously relapsed. You had relapsed over here, right in this apartment. And Ralph had been visiting, giving lessons at Billy's studio and invited him back, telling Matt, "I'll straighten him out. I'll take care of him. I'll look after him. Just send him home with me. Everything will be alright." And it was, according to Ralph, for six months. And then New Year's came. You were seen with a bottle of champagne. And you had hurt your back and were on pain pills. One nurse in the family said that often drug addicts who haven't used for awhile who have to take pain pills, start up again with heroin, because the painkiller ignites that whole memory in the brain, and they can't resist it.

YOUR MOTHER ERASES, CROSSES OUT, begins again, and finally has it down. Eme reads it. Matt reads it. Your father isn't even asked to read it. He wouldn't anyway. It's up to your mother if she wants to write it. Otherwise, he has already brayed out that the funeral parlor will take care of that. That's what they're paid to do. Meanwhile the television is ever present. The picture on the screen keeping everyone's eyes focussed off one another and on whatever comes on. The sound is muted during the commercials, and put on for the news, a show, the sports, anything of interest. They have their favorite newscasters. Your mother says how pretty some of the women are. She says you liked blondes. Jane Mattey is almost perfect in your dark-eyed Italian mother's estimation. "She's beautiful. What a face, and that color of hair...."

NIGHT FALLS AGAIN. Sleepless, haunted by memories, the subconscious drifting in and out of images, impressions. Matt wrapped around Eme in the narrow twin bed. Your mother and father sleeping side by side not touching. Matt going to her when he hears a sob, the silent floor, a carpet so soft and thick, you can walk without a sound. On hushed feet, Matt goes to his mother's side of the bed to comfort her to sleep and awake. He wants to be there at those moments when awareness strikes hard and deep, shattering any stability the nervous system gains as it gets upright and begins ritualizing its necessities of food, clothing, and shelter. Once your mother is awake and fussing over bagels in the kitchen, she will be okay. Then Matt can go take his shower and shave that Sicilian shadow from his face. He grew barbed wire to your baby down. Your beard was not much more than your mother's moustache. A fine silk thin hair. But you were the one devoted to chasing the women. While your brother could grow hair, thick and furious, but could have been a priest, for all the interest

46

he could muster up for sex—you were the opposite. He was always thinking. You were always feeling. It was the territory you staked out early, as brothers, for yourselves. You'd leave all the heady stuff for Matt to figure out. And he'd leave all the earthy stuff, below the belt for you to do. And it worked. You had the fun, he had the responsibility. Later, people would try to coin it as "dysfunctional." But it was functional. You went along like that for almost fifty years. Matt, turning 49 this summer when you would have turned 44. The war. Your mother said she had to wait five years for your father to come home from the war, to have another baby. Otherwise you would have been closer in age.

THEY TAKE THE OBITUARY down to the funeral parlor and come home silent. A solemn affair, even though there is a bit of writer's pride in your mother's countenance when she said in her contralto, "He said it was good; that nothing had to be changed." Tomorrow you will arrive in Los Angeles. A van will pick you up. It happens all the time. Dead bodies shipped by air back from all over the world. They've got it down to a science. Just like clockwork. The Home here will bring you back and prepare you for viewing. They will need your clothes. Matt does not want your mother to have to go through picking out an outfit. She sits in the chair now and wonders out loud what she should choose. She gestures toward the open hanging closet just on the wall above her bed. All your suit jackets and slacks neatly hung in plastic wardrobe bags. Your family does things right. It's part of the ritual your father has taught you. You preserve your clothing. You keep it nice. He has a sweater thirty years now that looks brand new. It's a point of pride with him, and so he taught you to spend the time to clean and arrange your clothes just so. Matt's shirts and slacks hang in the other bedroom closet as if they are on a rack at a men's clothing store. Immaculate, fresh from the cleaners, each hanging not touching the other, enough space between the garments so not to wrinkle them.

MATT ASKS HIS GIRLFRIEND, Eme, if she will pick out your clothes tomorrow when it is time to take them down, after you arrive in Santa Barbara. She is agreeable. In fact, she likes this part. Her curiosity is not polite. She will delight in any detail having to do with what's available and what the funeral people request.

YOU ARRIVE ON TIME. The clock on the wall of your family's apartment tells them that you should be here by now. You arrived in L.A. at ten A.M. And it takes two hours to drive you home. Matt watches the clock. Your mother watches the clock. The cuckoo clock goes off on the hour. They are so used to it, it goes unheard, but Eme nearly jumps out of her skin. It shatters the quiet. A quiet that is heavy ladened with unspoken words and unspilled tears, and fear of feeling what there is to feel. And, so it is, you are home. Your mother says it aloud. "Billy is home." And then she bends forwards and wails, muffling it. She so wanted you to come bouncing in through the door with your bright eyes and that smile. She pictured you a million times, your homecoming and how it would be. Your face full of mischief. That was the look you had. A naughty look. The look of loving and laughing and having fun, until you entered the apartment. Then you had to watch yourself. And that was the look she saw. The pretending to be a good boy, and knowing you weren't. You lit up your mother's face. You had her dark eyes. Matt's brown eyes were tinged with the blue of your father's eyes. And they were only priestly eyes. They had a Yoga glow, as if the spirit was within. But yours, you had that devil may care in them. And it excited your mother. At last someone was daring enough to live, even under your father's strict thumb. You were the only one who escaped him and kicked your heels up. Your mother was proud of you for that. What did she know. She didn't equate that with heroin. It was more like her Neapolitan family spirit. They were all musicians. She grew up in a quiet- spoken artistic family, the baby of eight children. There was music and singing and dancing and good feelings in that house. And then she married your dad. He grew up in a hard-working family where the father yelled out orders and criticisms from sun up to sundown, whenever he was around the house. He expected obedience from his wife and children and an eight-course meal every evening. His mother weighed three hundred pounds and never opened her mouth except to put food in. She finally never left the house. Her hard-working, tar-laying husband, who laid tar in the streets of New York City his whole life, ran the show. Your mother was not used to such force. She succumbed to it like a graceful reed in the wind. He bent her to his will. And she watched all through your childhood as he carried on in the male tradition of his family and brutalized his two sons with words from the time they were tots. She made no motion to defend them from words that sent them to their rooms intimidated. Maybe it was a bluff, just a role by example, that he played, but you and Matt were scared out of your wits of him as you were growing up. He was the first and last say about everything, while your mother performed her duties in silence. When asked by Matt now, your father doesn't remember that he ever yelled. He can't believe that you and Matt accuse him of that.

YOU DIED ON THE FIFTH of January, our time, which was really the sixth, Australian time. It was their Saturday night. They found you Sunday morning. They shipped you home on the fifteenth. You have been dead for ten days. The funeral home calls and talks to Matt in private. They say that your face is dark because of the length of time you've been dead. That perhaps a closed casket would be advised. That he should come look and tell them what the family wants. Matt comes off the phone with the primal scream look. A detail about your condition kills him. He nearly vomits up air in reaction to hearing the news, but stays out of sight of your mother. When he regains his composure, he comes into the livingroom where your mother sits in her chair, and looks up to hear who that was. He brushes it off as, "Just the home telling us that you arrived and everything is alright." Your mother goes on watching the O.J. trial. Then Matt, takes his girlfriend aside and explains what the home said. He says he will call Lydia and Hugh and see if they will be willing to go look and give the go ahead on an open or a closed casket. He makes the call and is stunned by their refusal. Hugh says that he doesn't want his wife to have to go through all that. Matt then turns to his girlfriend and asks her if she will. She is more than willing. It is the difference between blood and non-blood. This whole thing does not bother her. She will be of use anyway she can. But, her quickness in accepting to do it, bothers him. He calls up Rhoda, the wife of the attorney, a cousin, she is a nurse. She says she will do it. He tells her Eme will go with her and the two of them can decide. That they are to meet the next morning at the funeral parlor.

IT IS AN AGONIZING NIGHT. You are in town, just a few miles away now. The abstractness of being somewhere on the other side of the world falls away, and they are within reach. They have passed WelchRyderRice many times. The three homes merged about ten years ago and became one. It is by that big Catholic church, and near the park where all the festivities are held. Just last year you were walking by with one of your many women, a smile on your face, plans for fun, sex, rock 'n roll, good food, music. And there you lie. Dead. No one sleeps. Morning comes too soon. Eyes are swollen from not only crying, but from no sleep. Deep circles are visible. A haunted look predominates your family. They make their way through their morning rituals to groom and dress and go see you. Eme and Rhoda will let them know if that's possible. Matt is afraid. He keeps up a steady face for your mother, but doesn't want to go forward from this point on. There is nothing up ahead but something terrible, and he balks like a donkey on a hard rocky, steep and narrow trail along a precipice. If he should lose his footing now, what would become of your mother. It's a good thing he must protect her. it takes his mind off himself. Without her he would not know how to tailor the grief. He grieves now, as a protector, telling her it will be okay, that she will be okay. Grief has a form, a role, an image he can manage. He must be strong for her.

ON THE RIDE DOWN they take two cars. Matt and Eme go in hers and your parents go in theirs. Your father drives, being the head of the household, with your mother by his side. Her little knob of a head with the seatbelt stretched across one shoulder looks almost child-sized. She's always been a small woman, and now has lost weight and shrunk under the burden of your death. Later, she will learn that she has a bad case of survival guilt. Not only is the mother of her in anguish over no longer being able to nurture and protect her child, but to go on beyond him, in all the blatant organic ways one must go on, violates her appetite. Her humanity protests. It isn't right, and she cannot swallow food, thinking of your mouth filled only with your dead stiff tongue until the end of time.

ON THE DRIVE OVER, Eme becomes weary of Matt's sad demeanor. *Alright already,* is on the end of her tongue, but instead she challenges him with his bent toward Zen. She mocks his meditation sessions in her room for five years, and the sayings handbook tucked in her car visor which he refers to all the time. And now that there is something to transcend he can't do it. She goes on and on until he shouts her down with, "You are brutal"— to which she doesn't flinch. She ridicules the whole idea of you doing Yoga. "It's for the purpose of dealing with life on earth when it gets hard. It's easy to sit there cross-legged and transcend nothing. And then the dog dies and you worry that he'll take drugs. That's when he should use everything he's teaching. Why else do Yoga? It's for the barren, hard, meager existence in India. It was born out of coping with pain and anguish. And then the two of you cave in," she accuses, "when something real happens." Matt forgives her, believing it is her way of dealing with the stress of your death. She gets mad. She vents her opinions. It's nothing more than that.

YOU HAVE BEEN DRESSED. That was a fiasco in espionage. Matt covered the whole thing up so that your mother never knew when the clothes were chosen and disappeared from the house. As she sat trying to read the morning paper and watch the trial in one, you stole Eme into the bedroom and pointed to the closet. She was more than cooperative. She took to the task with interest, taking down each bag and eyeing the suits and sports jackets with her mind's eye alive with picturing you lying there dressed in this shade or that. Matt instructed her that the jacket could not be too dark or too light because of the darkness of your face. He chased your father out of the room. Eme took down all six plastic see-through bags and examined the blazers with great sighs of duty so that Matt could be comforted by them and not believe she relished the task at hand. He refused to look upon your clothes.

The vision of you wearing each garment at different family gatherings tore him apart. He averted his eyes and kept his face in profile while she laid the bags on the bed, tried to unzip them without making a sound, and leafing through them like shuffling cards. There was white, gray, light blue, beige, charcoal, navy, black. Wool, linen, gabardine. You were a dandy. When did you acquire and wear all these suits? Without a nine-to-five job? Without a white collar job? All you wore while teaching your Yoga classes were baggy drawers with a tie string. When Eme decided on two of them, she asked Matt to choose between them. She insisted that he finally look, so with great pain in turning toward the bed and seeing the clothes you would never wear again, he pointed to the lighter colored one. Your face was dark red, the man said, from falling forward and lying on it, face down, all Saturday night and until midday Sunday. All the blood had settled in it and it was supposedly as dark as a Concord grape.

YOUR FATHER PUSHED his way into the room and stood there glowering at what was going on. Matt took the suit and held it up while Eme put the bag away, hanging it on the rod with all the others. Your father blocked the doorway and cast an eye toward his wife sitting in her chair, with the question of how to get it past her. Eme simply folded it over her arm, folding it again, it was a silky kind of summer suit that could be tucked under her baggy sweater, which she did and then folded her arms over her stomach as if she were just walking, casual. Matt quickly grabbed a pair of dark socks and a white shirt from his closet, and then your father said abruptly, "What about boxers?" So

Matt took a pair of his and carried them all under his arm and kept that side of his body from his mother as they made their way through the livingroom to the front door. Your mother looked up absently, as if she didn't want to know what was going on. Later, she will ask, "How did you get his clothes?"

YOUR FATHER WAYLAID your brother's girlfriend on the way to the funeral parlor and asked why his son wouldn't tell him anything about the phone call, but would tell her instead. She explained that he wanted to protect him from what was said, of course. Your father shook his head. He said he was miserable being left out as if he couldn't handle anything. That Matt didn't trust him, and that he was the head of the family, had been through WWII and wanted to be let in on what the man said from the home. So, with hesitancy, she told him that she was not suppose to tell him, but she would and she hoped he wouldn't get upset over the information. And then she told him about the color of your face being dark, and why. She watched as his open face closed down with this fact, and then he brushed it all aside with relief, saying, "Is that all? I thought it was a lot worse. You know, if your son keeps something from you, your imagination goes crazy. So he got a tan over there. It was summer. So what."

AND THEN HE TOLD HER not to tell your mother. She couldn't take it, he said, just as Matt has said of him. And so the not telling this one or that one this or that for fear no one could take anything continued on into the funeral home where Rhoda was waiting.

RHODA'S MAKE-UP was as thick as if the mortician had made her up. It's as if she used a trowel and that her fair Irish skin couldn't be matched so that the contrast from the side of her face where the make-up suddenly stops and she doesn't blend it in, shows how orange her choice of foundation is to her pale skin. The make-up collects in her eyebrows and the hair along her loose jaw bone. And she pencils in some eyebrows in gray, and applies lipstick thick and dark, not seeming to care if it gets smeared above her lip. She is always in a hurry doing her face it seems, as if she has to get to work, and simply smears and splashes in the bathroom before the mirror. She works as a nurse for the elderly. Death is of no consequence for her. She sees people die almost daily, so that is why she agreed to look at Billy today. Eme greets her, Matt hovers by and then gives permission for them to go into the room and view you, Billy.

WELL, THERE YOU ARE. Sure enough. Dead. And just fine. Rhoda and Eme approach, saying to each other that you don't look as bad as they'd imagined by the funeral director's report. In fact, you look pretty good. You're not dark at all. They've evidently lightened your post mortem complexion with make-up, which Rhoda says is a bad job. Eme almost wants to laugh. It looks better than hers, actually. She should be a critic?

YOUR FAMILY STANDS THERE outside the viewing room, fearful, waiting for Eme and Rhoda to come out. They hold onto each other. You mother is in between your father and brother. She looks blank, as if she can't make sense of being here and you in there, and preparing to see you. Matt steps away and takes Eme and Rhoda off to one side where they discuss the situation of the color of your face. Rhoda says she would definitely suggest a closed coffin. But that she is a closed coffin type of person. She thinks it macabre to display a dead body. That the person you knew is not that dead person but the one you remember when they were alive. Eme argues that if they don't get to see Billy, his body, him, lying there, they will never quite believe he is dead. That it is important that they have an open coffin for this reason. As soon as they get used to the idea that there he is, and we now know it, the more they can settle with it somehow. That his color is fine. That she doesn't know why the funeral director thought it was too dark. Matt takes Eme's word for it, thanks Rhoda, and then goes back to your mother and father. They stand as if one foot is in a hole, crooked, somehow, bracing themselves and each other. Your father looks awkward hanging onto your mother, as if for dear life. To life. Who is holding who up? They have dressed up for the occasion. This is the day guests will be stopping by to pay their respects. They have come early to see that everything is alright and to have time alone with you. Now that you are all laid out and presentable, they will approach you as is socially acceptable. They want to do the right thing, and follow all the rules. This is a long time tradition, funerals are. Your mother found the obituary column early this morning and read about you, and held the paper to her chest and her face went all squeezed tight and wet. Matt had rushed to her and took the paper from her hand. He sat her down and petted her. Seeing the words she herself had written proved overwhelming. Writing it down was simply an exercise in following orders from the home. Now, reading it back makes it so. You are dead.

SO THEY HAVE COME TO SEE YOU, and your mother doesn't know what the holdup is. Why can't we just go in. She blurts out, "Billy's in there. I want to see him." Matt goes to his mother, and gives his father such a look, saying that Eme said the color was okay. Then he bends down into your mother's face and searches for words, "Do you want an open or a closed casket, Ma?" She flutters her old blue veined hands, wielding a tissue, and says, "What? Yes, open. Of course. I want to see Billy." And she wipes her nose even though it is still dry. All the movements of prostration are being practiced before entering the room where you lie. So, Matt leads the way, and then stops at the door he holds open and lets your parents pass. He refuses to go in himself. Eme urges him to. He plants his feet, and turns away. And then he is caught. He wants to be with his mother, yet he cannot bear to look. When he hears her bawling, he enters and goes to her side still averting his eyes, and then he looks. The three of them stand there like lost children in a storm at night. They are frightened and near to perishing themselves, looking upon your dead face. They have walked carefully up the aisle, your father's arm around your mother's shoulders, both the same height, and kept their eyes glued on you lying there in the shiny metallic coffin, on a white satin pillow. A bed. And you asleep. Except you look dead. Eme had called the funeral director in, before this, to have the lipstick corrected. it covered one side of your wide bottom lip and then ended, leaving the other side pale. The director disappeared in silence, as they do in these places, and reappeared with a tube of lipstick and a lip brush. He attempted to spread the color across your whole lip, but his hand was shaking and he did not succeed. There was only a little improvement, but she let it go.

RHODA HAD SAID to Eme "He just looks dead. He doesn't look like he's asleep. He's dead and they can't really make him look like he's at peace and all that like people say. " And now your parents stand just looking, their faces dripping, sounds coming of abject helplessness. They want you to open your eyes and smile and say you were just kidding around. But you lie there, a closed face, forever gone from them. Your eyes look sealed permanently. And your dark hair is theatrically combed in a big swirl back from your forehead. They can see where the make-up ends at your hairline and was meticulously wiped off so not to get on your hair the way Rhoda's is on hers. You look better than Matt thought you would after talking to the director that morning. As the visage of you overwhelms your small, short little parents who have to stand on tiptoe to reach you, they gulp and choke out grief, as if they are strangling. They begin to touch you. Your mother strokes your hair. She takes your hand and tries to hold it, but it doesn't come loose from the other one. She turns to Matt in a panic and says, "What's wrong? His hand is stuck. I can't hold it, it won't move." He gently takes her hand from yours and tells her in a nonchalant voice that it's okay. They put it like that. They pin them together. Don't touch them." His voice belies his primal expression of anguish. It is the worst point in his life. There can be nothing worse than this, and this has to be gotten through.

YOUR MOTHER CONTINUES to try to take your hands, and accepts the stiffness, and ends up just stroking them. She looks at your fingernails and fondly tells anyone, just says it aloud, "He always kept his nails trimmed so nice." And sure enough, your nails are trimmed just right. A flat, wide, rounded nail it is. A hand that felt many a woman, followed many a line of print in a book, pointed to many a thing while alive. And the same hands that took the needle that night and injected the deadly chemical into your vein. Capable hands, but without callus like your father's. Smaller hands than your dad's. They are not work hands. The skin is smooth as nice kid leather and porous in that Italian olive toned way. You can see the hairs jutting from the clean pores.

YOU HAD IT MADE, BILLY. Made in the shade of a Teatree oil Tree. Your mother brought the photos of you from Christmas. You sent the ones you took on a weekend vacation out somewhere in paradise. There's a swimming pool, vines, large tropical leafed foliage, beautiful people. Everyone tan and smiling and almost glistening from the good life. Bright colored bathing suits, good strong young bodies. And there you are standing under a light waterfall, holding onto a vine and grinning like a Cheshire cat. Looking 33 not 43. Whatta life. Six months of sheer luxury, even though you had to get some part-time work for pocket money. The man you worked for who owned the bar and cafe paid you eight dollars an hour to pass out flyers. He told Matt later that he could see the window of your room in that big two-story house from his bar. And sometimes you'd wave to each other. And that you would come on over, when the place opened and sit and shoot the breeze with him. He said you had plenty of girlfriends. But, when Matt questioned him further for any evidence of unhappiness in you, could he detect anything that might make sense of you going back on drugs, he came up with, "in the eyes, there was a look sometimes of worry or anxiety." Just fleeting, but that you never talked about any troubles or disturbing feelings. You mainly joked around and had a good time.

MATT WOULD TELL PEOPLE for the next three days of the long wake at the funeral home that you were "an innocent guy." "My brother was just an innocent kind of guy. He was so trusting and open." When it comes out six weeks after your death that there was some drug going around that was contaminated and you were just the first of a series of deaths of young people reported in the paper over there, it will crush your brother. He will picture you trusting and open-faced, buying the stuff, and walking home with it, "just an innocent guy wanting to shoot up just one more time for the heck of it. A guy who meant no one

61

any harm, ever." A simple guy. Not too complex. Just trusting that everything would work out. "He never expected this. And, in a way, he knew it could happen. He feared that he could die. He knew it was a risk. He had buddies that died of overdoses. But this probably wasn't even an overdose. We don't know yet if it was a combination or cocaine and heroin, or what. We have to wait for the report from the coroner. But he had been an addict since he was fifteen. You know? He knew what he was dealing with. But he didn't know this stuff was contaminated. They get it from Korea over there. And the dosage is stronger than here. Oh, well, what'cha gonna do...." And your brother would not know what to say or think after trying to defend you, describe you, so would shrug it all away.

YOUR MOTHER WANTS A LOCK of your hair. Eme offers to get a scissors from the receptionist in the waiting room. She comes back with a big office shears. The relatives and friends have not yet arrived. But just as your mother reaches for a nice strand of your hair, in the back so not to ruin the wave at your temple, people begin to arrive. She turns around with the scissors in her hand to greet her sister, Isabel. Isabel says, "What's this, what's this?" And your mother hands the scissors back to Eme, who stashes them in her purse until later, and never answers. They fall into each other's arms with grief. There will be plenty of time to take a lock of your hair. She took a lock of your dog's hair. Old Frankie, like the black and white border collie shepherd in that movie. A beautiful coat. He got compliments on his coat just the day before he died. And now you.

CLAUDIA COMES IN WITH HER SON. She was in love with you. She has been crying long and steady, or so her eyes show. No mascara. Naked eyes that look naked. Just sad and small things in the blue range, but not eyes you would remember. But eyes that followed you around when you stayed at her house. Eyes that adored you. Eyes that you got nothing out of when you looked into them. She was just one of your students who could bend into any position without strain. A rag doll. No bones. She came to all your classes and fell in love with you. A millionaire's daughter in her forties with two grown children, one with her now, and the other, a daughter travelling with her black athlete husband and their two young children. Claudia, a young grandmother, thin as a girl with no breasts. Her Mercedes parked outside next to your family's Toyota. A big car so plush and creamy colored that you expect a woman of some stature to emerge from it, but no, just little thin hippified Claudia in her Indian cloth pants and some tee shirt that shows only nipples on her bony chest. She sits on the board twice a year of her father's nationwide business of some electrical equipment that he manufactures for utility companies. And only three daughters. He pays them for being board members of the single family business. And she wants to pay for your funeral. She has already made the offer to Matt, who brushed it aside with, "We couldn't let you do that." So that she went to Eme and asked where the family was getting all the money to pay for two funeral homes and the shipping. She calculated that it was at least ten thousand dollars. More like fourteen, when she thought about it. Eme says she has no idea. That she knows nothing of the finances of the family even though she has been Matt's friend for over five years. Claudia and her son have brought a handheld bouquet without a vase. Isabel confiscates a vase from one on a table in the lounge, emptying it of the dry flower arrangement. Later the director will get angry over that and say they don't provide vases. But, Isabel, a rich woman herself, will stand her ground, and tell him they should then, because funerals don't come cheap. "After all they're paying...."

CLAUDIA HAD SAID IT WAS OKAY, "Just let them die with him. The flowers don't have to be preserved." She takes her stand beside your mother and just stands there, lightly touching the ground with her size four feet in some simple casual shoes. Her brown hair with gray is the same height of your mother. Your mother reaches out and holds onto her arm, and they cry silently at your side. You lie there. And people, as they come, begin to say the same old thing about you being in the room up there looking down knowing everything. Suddenly, you, in death, are attributed omniscient wisdom. You see all and know all and are everything you weren't in earth life when you were alive.

THE FLOOD GATES ARE OPEN. People are filling the place and everyone is shaking everyone's hands and then going to the bereaved and clasping them in heavy audible hugs and sobs. Matt goes for sobs to S.O.B.'s. He calls you a stupid son of a bitch for doing this and then sobs against the well-suited and upholstered shoulder of a big guy named Junior. Junior used to shoot up with you. He will try to put Matt straight about his guilt being out of place. "You did what you could, man, the guy was an addict. You can't do nothing to stop someone like that." Matt looks like a kid, standing chest high to Junior. Junior listens as Matt tells how your father used to yell at the two of you and intimidate you. Poor Billy, and he bawls out loud. The distraught face, eyes like pies, deep dish and crimped. But Junior won't buy it. He says, "You want to talk about fathers. You want to talk about abuse. I kicked the habit, and I had a father you wouldn't believe. Talk about abuse. My father was six foot four and weighed two hundred and eighty pounds, and I never wanted to be in the house alone with him. He used to kick the shit out of me. I mean I never knew when the guy would go off. He could go off in a split second. He'd be smiling one minute and the next, wham, he'd reach out and punch you down, and you never knew what you did to deserve it." Matt looks up, aghast. He's known Junior since grammar school. He lived right down the street. He grew up with you. You sat in parked cars in parking lots shooting up. And now he learns that Junior's father was worse than his.

LATER, ANOTHER FRIEND, a young half-Greek and half-Italian woman will tell Eme that she lived right next door to the Amatos and could hear the father yelling all the time. That she and you would play through the fence. And the big brother was Matt's friend. Her big brother, Lennie, has something wrong with his health now. He's bad off. And she gives Eme his phone number, because he would be able to tell her anything she wanted to know about Matt and Billy growing up. That she herself was too young at the time. And then they moved away. She just remembers Matt as very quiet and serious, and Billy fun and funny. Everyone, all the little kids her age, liked Billy, and they were all kind of in awe of Matt. "He never joked with us the way Billy did."

MATT ACCUSES ISABEL of "holding court." She is your mother's eldest sister who married well and had four sons who all took lovely wives and established beautiful homes all around her up on the hill overlooking the whole town and the Pacific Ocean. Old Uncle Mark there, now nodding off in his chair, came out from Long Island with an upholstery business back in the late forties when he was a young man and bought the whole hill, and as each son got married, gave him a lot; and all the sons and father pitched in and built each house in turn. It became a small dynasty in which Isabel was the Queen mother who put on such family celebrations that she was known for her parties all over. The special Italian dishes no one knew how to make. Now, the grandmother of fifteen grown grandchildren and the greatgrandmother of five with one on the way, she sits in the lounge and talks about her sons and grandsons and great grandsons, and all the beautiful granddaughters, as they come in the door to pay their respects, and give her the respectful kiss in the air by her cheek as they were taught. She is regal in her role, as if chisled in sandstone, and under her breath does not dare say what she is thinking, what shows in her careful eyes that pretend not to see what is obvious, that her poor sister had only these two sons, who didn't marry or have children, and that it is a

66

shame and now that one is dead, it leaves only the one, who has no plans to marry and bring a daughter-in-law into the family or a child, which would be or would have been a comfort for her sister. And that it is too late for grandchildren. You have grandchildren when you're in your fifties, not now, in your late seveties. Her face has the authority registering these implications about her life versus her youngest sister. She may tell how her own dear husband, Mark, over there, asleep and wetting himself at 90 offered Bill, her brother-in-law, a lot to build a house on right up there with all of them years ago, and how he turned it down to be in town where there was easy access to the clubs and stores. That even Jewell decided it took too long to drive down that winding hill to get to the main street to shop. A view didn't mean anything to them, the rolling hills with the swaying wild grasses by the blue sea beyond just represented entrapment. They were New Yorkers. They were used to East Forty-Second street type addresses, not up on yonder hill under that there oak near the great slab of sandstone before you get to the granite rock of the national forest. It did nothing to their aesthetic sensibilities. Sensibilities that were deveoped to see manmade achievement. A skyscraper higher than all the rest and so forth. And so Bill, your dad, turned down Mark, and rented the apartment that they've been in for sixteen years, paying almost a thousand a month all that time. Think of the equity they'd have in a house by now. Too bad. And now Matt even gasps at that. Perhaps you would be alive if they had bought a house instead of hoarding the money and calling it an investment by putting it in a bank and just having it. He rebukes your dad over that. He won't let go of

67

money. He likes it there. He didn't want to spend it. And you even used to laugh at him for it, picturing him a miser, surveying his bank statement and feeling snug and secure. The laughter was tinged with real ridicule.

BUT, TO YOUR DAD, the Elks Club and the hundred dollar a month membership to the Health Club was beauty to his eyes. He was a city man who was born into things already done up and ready to use. There was no pioneer in him. In fact, he never loaded his family in a car and went on excursions through your entire childhood. No trips. Ever. No camping out, seeing sights. Looking at nature. He worked, liked to be in his home and enjoy the fruits of his labors. There was no interest in his heart for discovering the world. Yet he goes, annually, to watch Christopher Columbus come in on the beach in that celebration across from the Red Lion Inn. He can take a little sand on his shoes, and then go back to the lounge for a drink.

STANDING ON A HILL next to Mark, his brother-in-law, and staring out across the ocean left him restless. So he set himself and his wife up in a nice apartment complex with a pool and grounds that were impeccable. They commenced to live as if on vacation for the rest of their lives. And, indeed, they were. He was retired from Con Edison after forty years. And he had the money from the sale of the house they'd lived in and paid off in Longmont, a suburb outside the city on Long Island. In those days the money was enough to buy into Santa Barbara, but he'd rather have it in the bank. And to this day, your mother groans that she wishes she had a house. She grumbles over the small kitchen. She compares it with her home on Long Island. "It was three story with five television sets, and three refrigerators. The boys' room was the attic, and it had a full apartment in the basement. The kitchen was magnificient. I had cupboards you wouldn't believe. There was a place for everything." And she sighs, tossing her arm in the small kitchenette she lives with now, within earshot of her husband, so he never forgets how he made the wrong choice, and how she is discontented. At this point, her husband looks down at the floor, shrugs through the room, says nothing, hoists about his muscular seventy-nine year old frame, which the Health Club used on their ad brochure for Seniors, with the big hands from carrying that tool box up and down tenement houses all over New York City for forty years. He has no comment.

SOMETIMES HE WILL GO get the picture of the house in Long Island, and show it to visitors, ignoring his wife's blame and sharing her pride. He will then describe the painstaking care in which he maintain his home. He will look up and whistle through his false teeth, how great the place was, with a look of shame that they ever sold it and for such a small price in those days after paying off the mortgage and putting so much of themselves into it. He has even gone so far as to explain the kind of breadwinner he was. He's sat people down and impressed upon them how he would pick up his check every Friday night after work, go to the bank, cash it, take it home to Jewell and after putting so many dollars in the seven envelopes he had laid out for gas, electricity, water, phone, garbage and any other heating costs, mortgage payment, insurance, property tax, food, repairs, he would give her the rest to manage in whatever way she needed to. She would take her two young sons to the department stores twice a year for their brand new seasonal outfits. They were fitted for suits, white shirts and ties, good pants, play pants, shoes. And, she herself would buy what she needed, including a coat with a mink collar, when mink stoles were the fashion. They managed so that they could afford to live in a respectable style. Jewell stayed home and Bill went off to work. Only after the boys were in high school, did Jewell take a job in a linen store as a sales clerk for a couple of years. She smoked. She drank dry martinis after work on a Friday night. They went dancing. She was heard to say that when Bill came a-courting, she looked at his shoes. That she judged a man by his shoes. And Bill was a dandy. His shoes were highly polished and without wear and tear. So she married him. He knew all the dancehalls with the big bands. He told Matt's girlfriend recently that Jewell was the only woman who smoked in those days. That she smoked young. He used to smoke, too. Did a daring young woman smoking before it was common excite him? Did it challenge him? Did he plan to get her under his reign? For years they smoked together. Only when Matt grew up and had his spiritual health-minded awakening did he talk them into stopping. By then they had had twenty or thirty years of it. That was the kind of household it was. The parents running things their way. The way of the working class in the new suburbs outside a teeming city. A city pulsing with music, drinking, night clubs, excitement. They would go into the city at night on a weekend and partake of the bright lights while they had their sons safely tucked away in suburbia where the school was just down the street, and the church just down the block. Their dream was to provide the good, clean American life for their children. Little did they know that one son would be born for the taste of all the excitement they'd moved away from. When he came of age, he headed for the streets of New York City and found all the fun, drugs, sex, and, instead of big bands, rock 'n roll. It was the Sixties.

YOUR FATHER PICKED UP THE TAB for the dinner that night. It was his funeral so he was the one to do it. He protested when your friend from Arizona reached for it. Horace made a feeble attempt to grab it while saying he didn't have any cash on him, but fished around in his wallet for a credit card. It was a point of pride that Horace lived well, and had just been transferred by his company from New York City, to distribute and manage the office in Arizona. He was always talking about his success, and big salary. He sold packaged meats. His company made big bucks selling nitrates in all the cured cold cuts they could distribute to stores in this West branch territory. He had money when it came to conversation, but now he didn't want to be the one to treat your family to dinner. He would sleep at their house and accept their hospitality, because after all, he had come over for their sake, not his. And, so he joked and laughed all through dinner. It was settled that your dad would be paying. The waiter was informed not to give the ticket to anyone but him. And your brother, Matt, sat poker-faced, not entirely agreeing on this plan. It

71

seemed he brooded that the responsibility should fall upon a guest, that they surely would try to alleviate the burden of your death in taking a family out for dinner, but he didn't fight your father tonight. He took Horace's word for it, that "It's on me tomorrow." Who knew if there would be a tomorrow, so he yukked it up, hilarious and talkative. Any word at the table ignited a story or a joke in his mind. And he ordered well, ate with appetite and drank like King Henry IV. And then everyone went home and to bed.

BACK AT THE FUNERAL HOME the next morning at ten A.M., your mother is saying, "In N.Y. it would be open at eight. Santa Barbara starts everything so late." Your father steers her in through the door by the elbow. She would just as soon elbow him away with a sharp jut of her arm as not. She allows him to escort her for propriety's sake. He is her husband, and this is what he does. And what she does. Even now. Even when the anger and blame are so deep and ready to strike, like the great cats in the jungle, just waiting for the kill. She walks beside him, and he plays his role at her elbow, always careful of not handling her too much. Why does he not protest her anger? Does he feel he deserves it? Is that one more family secret. What did he do to make her so mad. Just the yelling?

THEY CELEBRATED THEIR FIFTIETH wedding anniversary just four years before. A three thousand dollar affair. You remember. You were the emcee. You were modest and almost shy that night, holding the microphone and trying to get people out on the dance floor, to that band that sounded like the musicians were dying in their chairs behind their instruments. After all the hours your brother spent interviewing different bands and talking on the phone about what to play. "New York, New York," by Frank Sinatra. They even ruined that one. And no one was dancing. The Elks hall was too big. Finally you toasted your parents and said that your mother was the kindest person you knew, and that your father had worked all those years and all that overtime. That he never turned down overtime. There was some deep, knowing laughter to this one by some of the husbands in the room. Overtime? Did his paycheck reflect it?

THE BUFFET WAS SET UP on one side of that huge hall, with tables way over on the other side, and the band so far away leaving so much floor space, it was as if a thousand people would crowd the floor. A hundred people came. Mostly relatives. The food was healthy and basically vegetarian. Everyone ate heartily. And there was a sheet of cheese cake a mile long. You were in heaven with all that food. You'd lost ten pounds and had to have your pants altered that year. You were the picture of all things in moderation. Your Yoga classes were going well. You brought your checks home twice a week, made out to you from all those nice housewives and divorcees and a few Sixties men in drawstring pants still trying to get limber and tranquil thirty years after the fact. You showed those checks to your mother and father as evidence that you were capable of earning money. That Yoga meant money, not just some "alternative" lifestyle. You sneered that word in your father's face. The checks lay on the chair side table between your mother and father while they watched television. Like play money. And you a little boy.

PEOPLE BEGIN COMING IN AGAIN. The same ones. Claudia is first and has brought coffee and muffins this morning for your parents and Matt, herself and her son. Eme comes in late and sees that she has missed the coffee treat. You father offers her his last drop, and she decides to run out and get more coffee and pastries for everyone again, since they are sitting there with empty cups and everyone too polite to eat the last muffin. They have cut it into pieces with everyone eyeing them. She comes back with twice as much as Claudia brought and feels good about providing it, as guests come in and your parents can offer them something to eat and drink. Your parents needed a good set of daughters-in-law. What good are sons when it comes to things like this? Your parents have brought Norma's basket of fruit in the trunk of their car, but it will spoil before they will ever think to offer that to all the travel-worn relatives that drive up from San Diego, and down from Santa Maria. Again, this is their time to receive, not give, is in their manner. The two short and small parents of the deceased. They are the ones who are to be treated to things. How can they treat when they have been struck in the heart? It is in their body language, the impression they give

74

with gesture and tone of voice. In New York, in the old neighborhood, people would understand that. The house would already be filled with pots of food, casseroles, anything they needed so they wouldn't have to cook, and would have something to offer their guests. But not out here. One fruit basket. A morning of coffee and muffins. That's it.

YOUR AUNT ISABEL CALLS and announces that she wants them to come up for lunch. She has prepared rice and ravioli, meatballs and vegetables and salad. Your parents roll their eyes. She wants them to make the effort to go to her place way up there on the hill. It's always her show and they must bow, somehow. But not today. They can't make it. They are unable to get away. This is their day, their event. And, as the day opens up, and they approach the casket to look upon your deadness with each guest, each time, they cry as if it's the first time. They will not pull themselves away and go to Isabel's for lunch. They grumble awhile over how she would expect them to do such a thing at a time like this, and also tell it, as if it is a privilege that she has prepared food for them the way family is suppose to.

ISABEL BRINGS THE LUNCH to them. She enlists one of her four sons to help transport the kettles and pots of food. And soon the coffee table in the waiting room is set with plastic ware and paper dishes and a nice offering of homemade food. Your parents are taken from casketside and led out of the viewing room into the entrance where they are told to sit and eat. For your strength, Isabel says, and looks around as if for applause. Her grandchildren wait until Uncle Bill and Aunt Jewell have theirs and, because it is "Grandma," they fall upon it with real starvation, as if they have had only junk food since the last invitation home. They are a ravishing and ravished troop of body-builder granddaughters. All muscled out, scantily clad, and hair and lips blackened in the MTV hard chick style of the day. Old Isabel there would have been a hard chick if the hands of time could be turned back. She has the manner. Self-assured, trendy clothes, tough exterior. At one point she teases one of the guests who held a glass of water. "Oh, you like it straight up do you, ha." And he laughs, caught by surprise over her cocktail eyes.

THERE IS ONE GRANDDAUGHTER who is pregnant. She's the one you said was the most beautiful woman in the world to you. She is the fairest haired and has not dyed it black. Her only willfullness was to marry a Mexican, and a homely one at that. A tall awkward young man, darker skinned than usual, and with big over-sized teeth. He could play a Mexican underdog on T.V. There has already been a row over that marriage, but like everything else, it blew over and the family accepted it. After the funeral, she will begin to miscarry and give birth to a three and a half pound son pre- maturely. it will be after she cried so hard and long over you during the service and even brought the little friendship bracelet you gave her twenty years before when you first came out to California, to show Matt that she saved it all these years, that you meant that much to her. Her feelings surprised your brother. When she cried, he leaned into her ear and said he hoped "this" wouldn't be bad for her pregnancy. That night, as if his words seemed to trigger an early delivery, her baby was taken by C-section. That would have been two deaths. How death seems to draw people to it and propagate itself. She, full of life, and so impressionable that it stirs the fetus to be born too soon. Matt tells his girlfriend this, perplexed at the power of your death, and the intensity of everyone's grief. He will tell people how much you meant to people, but with a deadpan voice, not really believing they care as much as they pretend to. After all, what were you to them? So that this second cousin, who almost loses her baby, surprises him. Perhaps people are more genuine than he thought.

AT THE END OF ISABEL'S STAY, after she has one of her granddaughters help her clean up the lunch things, she asks Mark if he wants to see Billy. Their old Italian voices are like rough fond nudgings. "Mark," she calls several times, and goes over and touches him to wake him up. "You want to see Billy." And her eyes take in all he is about as he says, "Yeah." She turns and announced to everyone that Mark wants to see Billy. And then laughs. So she pulls on his old upholsterers hands, rocks him back and forth to get leverage, and up he comes with some effort. She has told it over and over, what her day with him is like. She must wake him up in the morning and get him out of bed. He doesn't want to get up. She talks him into it with her long-term mates phrases. She knows what to say. The weather is good. She'll make him something good to eat. He can watch T.V., a certain program. And then he budges.

She must bathe him, throw away the night diaper he wears, clean him all up. And all the while she allows him to keep his dignity. It is with compassion and love that she cares for him in this way. She will not have a home nurse come in. What would I do, then? she has asked. I like to take care of him. He took care of me all these years. He was a good husband and father. And she passes it all off as nothing at all but an honor.

NOW SHE TAKES MARK'S ARM and leads him into the chapel where you are lying, doing what Mark wants to do for the rest of his life. Just sleep. Even at ninety, the old eyes shoot to your corpse with utmost interest. Death is an attention getter, even when you think a person is too feeble to take it in. They make their way up the aisle between the pews and old Mark is stationed right there looking down upon your dead face. He looks, kind of nods. Sure enough it's true. And the dark of his Italian eyes reflect light in a certain wetness around their rims. He doesn't cry, but he knows. And what it is he knows, he is keeping to himself. Then he smiles ever so faintly. To him you are in pure peace and restfullness. Is it envy? He gazes at how you will never have to get up again and try to go through another day for no reason except that you are still alive. Ah, how sweet death is to old Mark. It won't be long before he can just lie there like that with white satin billowing all around him and sleep til the end of time. After a long stand and gaze, Isabel, who has studied her husband's response, says it's time to go. She turns her man, a solid bull-bodied male, pasta-fed and nearly dead, and takes him back the way they came, and they bid the mourners farewell. She must take Mark home. She can tell he is tired; she announces it like the queen mother taking the king off to his chambers after the ball.

MARK'S ALCOHOLIC SON and his wife come to pay their respects. Old Dylan, who almost died last year of a heart attack and had to have his arteries rerouted with veins from his legs, will not go forward to see you. He eyes the whole funeral scene, and everyone holding everyone and sniffling, as something he prefers not to think about, be a part of or even admit it's a fact. "Ain't none of us getting out of life alive," still haunts him, after Peter Fonda said it on the Johnny Carson Show twenty years ago. A rude awakening, even if he was thirty. He stands in the back kind of swaying, and more sober in his demeanor than he's ever been. He sends his alcoholic wife up the aisle to pay respects to the congregation around the casket. She comes smelling of booze, smiling as if it's a party, and tells your parents that they had to give up going to a rowing meet that their son was in to come here. It is another way of trying to say, look, we care enough to do the right thing. If Billy was so stupid as to ruin his life, we, at least have taken time away from what we really want to do to come here, to put in a showing, so don't fault us on it. And know how we sacrificed just for you. Dylan, who is known for his sarcastic remarks, keeps his mouth. He will not utter even a sympathetic statement. It's as if he's mad and scared. That that could be him, and probably will be in the not too far future. At the rate he's going.

BEFORE THE DAY ENDS, people begin to want to put things in the casket for you to take with you into the forever after. Claudia brings a small white teddy bear and asks your mother if she can place it by your shoulder. It leans against the make-up on your face, and later she exchanges it for a brown teddy bear. Your mother places Isabel's rosary beads in your hands. Do you need to say them now? Isn't that to prevent death? But, nevertheless, they are wrapped around your fingers. At one point your mother comes to talk to you by herself and sees the brown teddy bear. She begins to be frightened and turn and call out, "What? what?" And Claudia rushes up and explains how she wanted the white teddy bear with your make-up on it to keep and traded it for the brown one. You mother almost laughs. She waves her hand and says how she didn't know what was going on. That perhaps there was something happening because of you. That you could change the colors. Claudia pats her until she has calmed down. Someone suggests your dog, Frankie's ashes should be brought and placed beside you, and so it is, and everyone can see the urn there, that cost a hundred dollars from the Humane Society who did the cremation, with his name on it. So you are all set to go where people go when they die, armed with love tokens and such. And then one woman steps forward. She is the wife of the sitar player. Remember that evening when he played and everyone brought health food, all those New Wave types, and sat on stones and listened to that ancient intrument being strummed at that beautiful Montecito estate? Well, you must have said something once to them about fathering a baby way back in the Seventies, because she asks the permission of your mother to place an envelope in with you, and tells her to please not read it. As soon as the woman leaves, your mother goes off in private and reads the contents of the note inside. It says, "Billy, Isn't it too bad you never saw your son? Aren't you sorry you never got in touch with him?" It was like dropping a bomb in the middle of the mourning. Your mother's heart jumped, and she quickly found Matt and handed it to him asking what it meant. He's a sly guy. He passed it off as nothing and that he doesn't know. And so your mother lets it pass, but not without saying she is sorry she ever read it, wondering if there could be some truth to it, and then shrugging and taking Matt's word for it. She's lived her whole life not rocking the boat. So why not now?

YOUR SECOND COUSINS, they all look alike, Rhoda and Mark's five beautiful daughters, with either flaming red or darkened black heads of hair, with body-builder bodies in black tights and tank tops, or elastic tit huggers and mini skirts or underwear worn as clothing with black stockings and boots, come and go. Their hair, long, moussed up or down, and swung off the shoulder, behind the ear, every which way that is enticing, showing their earrings, lily-stemmed necks, cleavage. Black lipstick. Purple lipstick. Heavy eye make-up. And a manner as if they are on their way to something else and are just passing through and have no time to say much. That one, the second to the oldest, gets stuck at the door leaving, saying goodbye to Eme and tells her the story of her worst relationship. She tells her as a way of saying she knows about heroin addiction. That she didn't know you were a user, but that her ex-husband was an addict. She sympathizes with Matt.

"WHEN YOU TRY TO INTERCEPT an addict, your life is a living hell. You live on edge with them. You never know when they are going to use. No one in my family knew what I was going through. I was just like Matt. I didn't want anyone to judge him or me, so I pretended everything was fine. But it was seven years of the worst nightmare of all time. I dated him and knew he was doing it, but thought I could cure him. He was sneaky, a liar, a cheater. All his money went for using. I couldn't turn my back without his disappearing, and I never knew when he would come back. He'd go on a binge, and then be sorry and promise he'd give it up. And everything would be fine for awhile, even though I couldn't relax, and then, he'd be gone and I'd go looking for him and find him all strung out at his friend's. I even threatened that whole roomful of jerks. I told them I'd turn them in, but nothing helped. I married him, thinking that would help. But we got divorced in a year. He was a nice guy. I really loved him. He's an artist. It broke my heart."

AND THEN SHE'S GONE. Eme stands there stunned. The girl looked as innocent and inexperienced as a doll. And she'd been through that. No wonder she hugged Matt with such warmth. She knew.

YOUR WAKE BROUGHT OUT the serious side of your family clan. While, before, at any holiday gathering, the fifty-plus husbands and their wives talked silly, making fun of one another, jabbering just to hear the sound of their voices when they were boozed up enough, now they strained to say something of meaning. And it was hard for them to switch gears. They'd spent their lives being light-hearted, never tackling any weighty topic. As, your brother, Matt explained to Eme when he took her to the first family party, a New Year's, "Now, these are just blue collar workers. They aren't intellectuals. They don't talk subjects. They all just stand around and bullshit. It's just their way. I don't think I've ever heard an in-depth conversation at their houses ever."

NOW THE BRUTES and their hard chick daughters, and the few sons with wives of their own, are brought up short. They come through the door with straight faces instead of the usual grins, and hold their tongues from making the same old wisecracks about how stupid everybody is, and stand around speechless. When going through the motions of courtesy they make perfunctory statements, shy for the first time. A kind of mimickry of sympathy. You see their jugulars and adam's apples bobbing, suppressing the lightweight humor that they are accustomed to speaking. They have never shown their serious side in public. They keep that private. Now they are forced to dig into their own experience related to the subject of death by overdose and make a statement appropriate for the occasion, to your family. They become confessional. Confidentiality takes the place of talking about "life" and then death. They clap Matt around the shoulders and hug him like a brother and use their utmost capacity for thinking of something nice to say about you, Billy. They escape with the whites of their eyes showing, giving sidelong glances as they exit, relieved to be through with it.

DEATH IS NOT WITHIN THEIR SCOPE at the present. They are starting businesses of their own, working out, getting things going for a long and costly future. This ultimate stopping in one's tracks is outside their reality. How could Billy have ended his life when theirs are making such strides. The energy taking them up into the next income bracket, and forward toward more opportunity, is such a force each day that it is difficult to comprehend an end of all that. They blink over the abruptness and finality of your death. And especially you. You were full of life. You made them laugh. You were cool. Now, Matt. There's another story. We could believe it if he died. So shut down he is. And grim with all that vegetarian stuff.

THE DAY ENDS ABOUT SIX. The last of the people wander out, saying their last condolences; and even in your mother's anguished state, she motions toward one wealthy woman leaving, telling someone that this woman buys all of her clothes in Beverly Hills. That her hats cost a couple of hundred dollars each, and she is never without a hat. We study your mother, to see where this came from. We thought she was taken over completely by your death. But there was that glance, that eye, and her words to defy us. Claudia and her son linger behind and are invited to dinner with Eme, Horace, your parents and Matt. As Claudia and her son drive away, again, your mother points out how expensive is the car she drives. "A Mercedes, brand new." And she adds, "Billy said she told him she would give him anything he wanted." And raises her eyebrows for the first time in the Old World way of suspicion and enticement.

84

LATER, MATT WILL INVESTIGATE where you got the money to buy heroin. About a thousand a day to use, he will tell Eme He will ask Claudia how much money she gave him totally over the year she knew him. She will say that he asked for twenty once, and she gave him two hundred. And another time she gave him five hundred. And then when he came back for more and began expecting it, she asked him, "What do you give me? Why should I give you anything then?" And that was the end of it. She was in love with him and he wouldn't return it. She told your family that you were never romantic with her. At your funeral, she offers to pay for the whole thing. She tells Matt that would make her happy to do so. She asks Eme if your family can afford all this expense. Eme pretends she knows nothing of your family's financial situation. She only remembers your property in Colorado with a river running through it that they might sell to pay for your funeral. Matt told her it was worth a hundred thousand dollars. But they wouldn't let you sell it and have the money when you were alive. It was "an investment property." You hold onto it for the future. Wait for the top dollar. So you went around broke except for teaching Yoga. That's where Matt wanted you, earning your own way.

THIS TIME THEY GO to your father's favorite place, Andreas. It's Italian and along the waterfront. The table is long, menus big and stiff, and everyone can see that it is more expensive than last night's place. Horace takes a look and loses any appetite. It is his turn tonight. And there are more people. One of your friends, Leroy from Newport Beach, a guest of the family, has arrived. Horace's voice drops, and he looks pea-soup green around the gills, as he looks down the price side of the menu. He mumbles his order, and braces himself as the waitress takes everyone's orders. He looks with some contempt, and no humor, at your parents as they bicker over which fish dish with what pasta to order. Last night their arguing and doing their schtick was comical. Tonight, he can't crack a smile.

YOUR FATHER IS TIRED OF CRYING over you. He wants to head the table with merriment. He orders wine and starts insisting everyone drink up and talk and laugh. He says why can't we have a good time even at a time like this. Your mother holds her glass up for the cheers. Claudia has another bottle of wine delivered to the table. From that point on your parents dote on her and her son. More wine. More food. Anything. And she beams, as if she is your beloved widow, and their favorite daughter-in-law. She keeps her little eyes on your father as he talks and gets her to laugh. He gets around to telling the story about the night of the blackout in New York City. How he was working late and had to go out to a certain Latino quarter of the city where the wire had been cut down in the basement so the tenants wouldn't have to pay their utility bill. And the little boy waiting out in front sees him and calls up to his mother at the tenement window, "La luz, la luz."

SO, THEY LET HIM IN and he goes down into the basement and sure enough the wires have been cut, so he fixes them, and the lights come on all over, and the little boy cries again, "La luz, la luz." And then, as he's putting away his tools, all the lights go off. He tells how he took a look outside and there was not a light on for miles. It was pitch black. And how he got worried and wondered if he blew the whole city out, and had to call in to find out if he did, and they told him that there was a blackout from some other place. There is laughter all around the table, except for Horace. He seems not to have heard the story as he chews his modest portion of food.

IN FACT, HORACE HARDLY SAYS A WORD all evening, and when the bill comes, and your father grabs at it, he lets your father win again. At that moment, with the bill in your father's hand, the weight is lifted from Horace's spirit, and he gets bilious. The red comes back to his complexion and he fills out. He breathes an audible sigh and explains what has made him so quiet tonight, that he was just tired, and apologizes for being no fun. But, he has spoken too soon. Matt gets up, walks around the table, takes the bill from your father and hands it over to Horace. Horace's smile hardens into a grimace as Matt preaches to your father, "Let someone give to you once in awhile." All the other guests at the table freeze to show no reaction to Horace's predicament. and be expected to offer to help. All eyes are turned toward Horace as he reluctantly takes out his credit card, and the cash he claimed he didn't have the night before comes bulging out so that he must pat it back inside. He spills the rest of his credit cards, and fumbles getting them back in. As everyone gets up and meanders out, clapping one another around the shoulders, remembering this dinner was all about your death, Horace looks like he's on a leash. He shows no bones, and his head is bowed, shoulders rounded. Is he remembering all the times he let you stay at his place free and gave to you?

IT WILL BE A RESTLESS NIGHT. You will be put into the ground tomorrow. Your mother and father, Horace, Matt, Eme, and Leroy, Claudia and her son, stand around in the parking lot saying goodnight and hugging one long last time before the big day.

AND ARE YOU JUST FINE? There in the dark with the place locked up? Is there a night guard? Are there still bodysnatchers? Is it that poor sap who told us to leave our food on the coffee table and he would clean it up, and if we wanted to leave any for him he'd eat it, still there? A hapless chap with crooked teeth, too tall for such a boy's manner, and a blotched complexion, as if the mortician had had a go at the broken capillaries along the cheeks and nose. Hey, Billy. What's it like, lying there dead instead of home with your family right now? Just think, you could be lying on your back in one of the twin beds next to your father right now. You could be watching your manners and walking on eggs, or screeching back at him, like some caged monkey if you'd just come home as planned. What'd you overdose for anyway? To escape a life worse than death, or what, man. You didn't have it so bad. You gave your family a run for their money. You'd have escaped again, you know. So, what's it like now, being dead. Is this any fun? You look really stupid, man, really stupid lying there and everybody knowing what you did to get there. Whatcha doin' man... Ah, shit....

THE BIG DAY HAS ARRIVED. Your mother pulls herself from her bed like she's stuck in mud. Gravity tugs at her old body making her walk like a coolie under a yoke with bowed legs and bended knees bearing the weight of your death. It is the heaviest thing she has ever carried. When she carried you forty-three years ago she thought you were heavy. She gained thirty pounds. And she's a small woman. What, not even five feet? Now she carries you in her heart and you weigh in at about a ton. She drags herself to the bathroom. She drags herself to her room to dress. She finds her black bouse and skirt. Yes, she will not break tradition today. At Eme's father's funeral, she wore summer shorts and a tee shirt. But he was an old man and no one she knew very well. So she is capable of being light-hearted at a funeral. But not today. And she is on display, like a bride. Everyone will be looking at the mother of the dead son. Too bad you never let her be the mother of the groom. There were so many women who wanted to marry you, even without money. Maybe because you didn't have any. Women are that way. Their hearts go out. And you apparently had something else to offer. Those dark eyes with the devil in them. That toothy smile that went all the way across your face from ear to ear. Flashing white like an actor on stage. You had something. How were you in bed? A lover type? Must have been, true to your Sicilian blood? Or, the thought of that alone turned the women on, or what?

YOUR FATHER BREATHES SO AUDIBLE in great sighs of impatience and duty. Your death is such a damn bother. He has to feel. He has to deal. It's thrown off his whole daily routine. It's interfered in his life, and now threatens to change everything. His wife will never be the same. He has no access to her anymore. You fill her heart and he can't intervene in this thing she has going with you now. His one living son will never be the same. He will never be the same. And he had things going pretty well before you did this stupid thing of killing yourself accidentally. He is seething and grieving. A dominant male and a father. The two do battle inside him moment to moment. He doesn't know which one to be. As he dresses, he reminds himself that he was a soldier in WWII. That he knows about death. That he never thought it would hit so close to home. But, whatcha gonna do? His step is unsure, as if he's in quicksand and it's too late. He's been tricked somehow. How'd he get here? It's a dangerous place to be in.

MATT DRESSES THE WAY HE WOULD dress for any family gathering. He wears the same pressed slacks, white shirt, good shoes. The only difference is that he puts on a dark jacket and tie. The whole process of dressing for your funeral is blasphemous. His manner and face show the drudgery of recognizing such an unearthly deed with mere animal hindquarters and no true spiritual contact. There should be some other way to do it, he feels. He, the reader of Eastern religious thought. How do you mourn? What do you do? Maybe ashes and sackcloth would be right. There should be something else. Not just dressing in regular clothes and going down there and putting you in the ground. Why doesn't the world stop and take notice. How can people just be walking past the funeral home and ignoring the fact that you are dead. How can you be so insignificant to everyone but him and your mother and father. Why doesn't the sun go out for the day. He is perplexed and expresses his surprise to Eme, who listens as if to gather ammunition she can shoot back at him later. She has tried to use your death as a teaching mechanism for your brother. A low blow to point out all that is wrong in his life now that he is vulnerable enough to listen, and maybe assess your death by it. She's had a dose of your family. After sleeping over for a week, she now sides with you. You were right to get the hell away from those three. They'd drive anyone nuts with their nitpicking life style. Horace and Leroy, the house guests also dress. They take a separate car and head out together out of ear shot of the family, where they no doubt pass commentary about everything they've been holding in. Do they breathe a sigh of relief to be out from under the roof of that household where there is no let-up on your death. Every moment is ladened with it.

Leaden with it. Billy is dead. Dead. No longer going to come home. He is here. And he is dead in that casket. And we will put him in the ground today.

MATT MEETS EME in the parking lot of the funeral home. She sees he is stricken more today than when he first heard. At first there was so much business to attend to, and he, a businessman. He passed the ten days with the phone in his ear. And now he's here facing all the preparations he made. There is nothing more to do but let the great mechanism grind its way forward, plowing you under, as is the way its done. He must stand aside now and watch life takes its course. He must be passive and let it happen to him. He has spent all his time, up to this minute, arranging things to happen his way. He has felt he was happening to life. He had the bull by the horns. And it is hard for him to let go. It feels feeble. He feels ineffective. He is embarrassed. There he is, the big brother, firstborn, the responsible one, just standing around like everyone else letting his brother be buried, after letting his brother die. He keeps inserting himself in your life, making himself the key character. He gave himself the major role, and now he's been put aside and told he doesn't count. He is no longer needed. That this thing is bigger than he is. So he stands with Eme, squinting in the sunlight of the bleak parking lot, milling toward the door with everyone else. Just being one of them. The reduction of his purpose plays on him. He tells Eme he feels unreal. She snaps back that it is the first time he is real. That, finally, he must just be a human being caught up in the human predicament and to respond to it without some electronic device or activity between him and reality. Her words are just words to him. He used to marvel at her sharp tongue and wonder how she felt she had the right to slash to the bone, but learned that she doesn't mean anything by it. She simply must say what comes to her mind, and her mind works in insights quick as lightning, and then they're gone. He's gotten used to it. It isn't the way his mind works. As a bachelor, he was inexperienced in women in general, stayed to himself most of the time, and never knew a woman could just let go with a barrage of words the way Eme did. But, he's learned to handle it. He simply doesn't say anything back. That sometimes stops her. The few times he tried to defend his position, it stimulated her so, that she monologued for half an hour without taking a breath. It's in her family. They are that way. Tact is not part of their learned behavior. The right to enlighten people without anyone's permission, just because you get a reading on the truth of the matter, is all the validation they need.

THE FAMILY AND FRIENDS troop into the funeral home and are seated in that terrible hush that lurks in places like this. Billy, you seem to float today, above us all. It's been three days, now, looking upon your deadness. The director of the home told one guest that he has never had a funeral like this. He remembers funerals like this as a kid back in Minnesota where the family would have the body of the deceased in the house and everyone would come and bring food and view it for a week, and get used to it, and then have the burial. He has not had a family yet, stay at the funeral home from ten in the morning until ten at night taking guests for three days. He went off, wiping his brow. It was more commotion than he could take, watching the place with those furtive eyes and gestures. The quiet of the home completely dismantled. The bathroom used over and over again, the waste baskets filling up in the course of a day. The other mourners who had their dead relative, sitting on the periphery of this large social occasion, looking askance. No one wanting to even swap stories about who in your family died compared to who in mine did. Pretending not to overhear all the stories being told by the visitors of your family about you. Billy this and Billy that. They came in waves. Your whole life conjured up. Each phase revealed by whatever friend arrived with their own capsule of memories.

ONE, MASON, WOULD MAKE YOU MAD. Maybe you're turning over in your grave, as is said. She comes in with her blonde curls standing on end and her round blue marble eyes almost cyclopic. She is sure you committed suicide over her and wants Matt to go to a seance and have a psychic channel you in to tell him the truth of your death. She goes on about how passionate your love life was, but that when she learned of your drug habit, and your behavior displayed erraticism, she had to think about herself and leave you. She must be myopic, standing not more than three inches from Eme's face and, without blinking for half an hour, swells with the story of your nine-month love affair. She clutches a tissue she never uses. Her pink lips quiver, however, in some emotion, maybe not related to your death, but to her nerves over the performance she must put on for everyone. We all knew it hurt you to break up with her. And now, she, the culprit, has arrived. All eyes are on her, and she's a primadonna anyway, like you. She's before Yoga classes all week in her little g-string outfits, with that narrow torso as strong as a horse's neck.

AFTER THE FUNERAL, everyone is invited up to your cousins Hugh and Lydia's. She's preparing most of the food, but potluck dishes are okay if people really want to. Those second cousins are into Thai food. The hot dishes will begin to arrive before your body settles deep and sound into the satin lining of the silver casket. Funerals are a kind of celebration, to be sure. Everyone knows all they have to do is go through the service with a somber face and then follow one another up the hill and feast. They file in and find seats in the pew of their choice. Some relatives prefer the back if they weren't too closely related to you. Your mother's niece and her husband and their friend, for instance. And others, the ones living in town, try to sit toward the front to show their respectful position in your life. Your parents and brother, of course, are seated in the front row with the two house guests, Horace and Leroy. Your Aunt Isabel settles in beside her baby sister for a long session of serious tears. She, the elder and the matron of that family. She has buried all her brothers and sisters, except her youngest beside her now, and her parents and one granddaughter. She has a box of Kleenex in her lap. And you are just fine. You died happy by all reports. You lived up to the last minute with your devil-may-care spirit, and died by it. And there you lie, into eternity. Truely transcended now. In the state of Nirvana at last. And you couldn't care less about the roomful of weepers. Your eyes and lips are sealed. Forever.

A MAN IN A DRESS COMES OUT with a long necklace dangling down to his belly with a cross on the end. For those not Catholic, he looks silly. In fact, even for Catholics he looks silly because he is too young, fat, and one of those kind of sissy types tough boys like to pick on. He looks like he went into the papastry just to hide from them. And he has a speech impediment. But, of course. They all do, and it's passed off as a kind of religiosity enunciation, sounding like old English, or Hebrew, or Sanskrit if it were spoken. It reminds us of all the licentious sex priests in the news, currently, have with their mouths. All those little boys finally telling on them. So it seems appropriate that this misfit is a priest. That a probable sexual deviant shrouds his privates this way. All the onlookers take in the spectacle of him without a sign that they see anything at all but a priest. In fact, your mother will think he was "very good." That he is simply the priest who is a substitute for the one they wanted. Old Father McQuaver, who knew you well, couldn't make it. He's too important in this town anymore. He is the old one who married Matt at the Mission years ago. Matt, at 35, his wife only 22. It lasted maybe five years, three living together and two in wedlock. It was back in the hippy days in Venice, California. They had a little tiny house. A cute wooden thing near the beach. After the divorce, the family sent all their photos to the lab and had her brushed out. Eme had wondered why some photos looked a bit blurry next to Matt and the landscape didn't fit. When Matt told her that, she thought of the Mafia. Being "rubbed out." And you guys were very Italian, and could play in a movie about the Mafia. Everyone said so. The two of you, you and your brother moved your bodies and turned your head at the same time. Seeing the two of you together made people smile at first, and then laugh out loud. You never knew how much you were brothers in that sense. The same height, mannerisms, constricted affect to cover your behinds. Your father wore a sweat shirt at times that said in Italian, "Don't break my balls." You went around together with that written on your faces, passed down, no doubt, from your old man. You walked like him, chest out, arms ready to swing to protect yourself, chin up. A kind of strut for such a small stature. Good shoulders. Built the way a man is suppose to be built, the torso tapering down just so to the hipbones.

THE CATHOLIC PRIEST behind his pulpit now is definitely not Italian. He is as new and green, an American Irishman as they come. He has his words all laid out before him on paper in case he forgets his lines. He never knew you. He begins the way they all begin, about you being in good hands and how the rest of us are the ones who should be worried. That you were a good guy and went to the right place and now your troubles are over. He recites the right Scriptures, and then announces that instead of saying ten Hail Marys for each stanza, the family had requested that only three be said. And the service drones on with a few voices standing out, saying even the priest's lines along with him. There are some true believers in the audience. And, an audience it is. The priest performs his duties, plays his role and makes your parents feel better like any actor. You are now out of their hands and in God's, he tells us. They are skeptical but your father has his "whatcha gonna do?" look on his face. All they know is that you will never again come home, and no matter where you are, if there is a Hereafter, it doesn't do them any good right now. They sob loud and clear. Others join them. And then it is time to stand up and bid you farewell before the coffin lid is shut. Someone holds your mother up, and another big relative takes your small strong father by the arm and aids him as he clasps at the casket, almost knocking it over. The stand rocks and the priest turns away to get the director, who hovered nearby. He is clearly embarrassed by your parent's unleashed emotion. His words obviously didn't mean a thing to them. You mother tries to hold onto you with all her might. It is her sister, niece, and Lydia who pry her hands loose and lead her away. She is easy to lead, a docile woman, who will confess much later, when all the blaming begins between the three remaining members of your family, that she is sorry she didn't provide a better father for you, that she was too passive all these years. And then the lid was closed, and in a matter of seconds, they had you carried out to the hearse. The simple wooden frame your casket had been resting on looked like the party was over. Just a bunch of sticks without the decorative silver grey casket. The few chosen relatives and the one house guest, Horace, from Arizona, were to go in the limousine. Old Uncle Mark was helped in beside Isabel. He couldn't make the step and missed the seat and was caught on his back unable to get up off the carpeted limo floor. All the men tugged at the old bull, and put him in a sitting position. All the while old Mark had a grand time. Finally something was happening. The monotony was over. He was living again. Isabel fussed, and everyone looked away, making their polite family jokes about wanting to pull a little trick on them, and they were off. Eme took her car and ran out of gas in the procession. She barely slid into an Arco station and refueled, making her late at the cemetery. Everyone was gathered, their skirts and pantlegs flapping in the breeze, the grass so green after the flood that it startled the eyes. Flowers standing in pots all around, and the same priest saying something to the wind, holding open a book, and waving his hand ever so gently. And Eme's car comes creeping up the gravel road and parks with its slipping bands behind the last car. There's Matt, your mother and father, all the cousins with their red hair and black lipstick, friends and distant relatives all perched in the wrong shoes in that deep grass, trying to hold still and listen to the last words before you would be lowered down. And there's your casket perched above the gravesite, sending a star off into the bright sun, the light glinting off the silver metal.

STANDING THERE was the hardest thing your mother ever did. She leaned heavily on everyone. And she was confused. Your father tried to steady her, but his own stature was sagging and off balance. They didn't want to be here doing this. Every cell in their bodies was protesting. Fall, faint, die, run, beg, beat the ground, look helpless, dissolve, bellow, moan, wail, rage, rant, groan, shake your head no,

99

no, no. But the big machinery grinds them into itself and they take it. They take your death. They hear all the words, and see all the sights on display at your funeral, and they get through it. They are helped back into the limousine as soon as the priest's words stop. It is enough. It is over. One last bang and pound with their old hands on your three thousand dollar casket, and they give up, give in, and leave.

MATT STAYS BEHIND AND FINDS EME. He searches her face for something. She watches his like a science experiment. Old Lucille comes up with her sallow friend with the earring. She used to shoot up with you in Venice. She called it "partying." She knew you well. Now, she has an ex-husband, a ten-year-old son, and a new boyfriend. It turns out he is from Australia and wants to tell Matt all about Paddington, the suburb of Sydney, where you spent the last seven months of your life. Matt is in a daze. The words slip by him like the breeze. He has just buried his brother. You. And he can't believe it. This is exactly what he was trying to prevent all these years. And now your casket is about to be lowered. The grave-diggers are standing around. They want to finish their work and get on to other things. They wait politely like birds of prey, dark, even bald, eager. How many funerals have they seen? Do they get bored with families standing there crying over someone in a box? Has it all become so commonplace that they have their inside jokes? Each family predictable but with their own style. This a rich one, that a poor one, the other an educated class, another heathen. How do they see the public as we come in to bury our dead. And does it effect the way they respond when one of their own die? There's a book that could be written, but what of the sacrilege?

MATT MILLS OFF, taking Eme by the arm as if she is his mother, and steers her toward her car. He will drive up the hill with her. Hugh and Lydia left the funeral service a little ahead of everyone to prepare for the arrival of the funeral party. The long table has been set with all the casseroles and salads, slices of meat, and bowls of prepared vegetables. Your picture is stuck to the refrigerator by a magnet for everyone to see. It's just a small snapshot they took of you visiting once. Your wide smile, the dark eyes with that double-take expression from the Sixties, like wow. You're in a tee shirt and shorts. Your arms and legs are tan. You look easily alive. So easy to be alive when you're not dead. It boggles our minds. There you are, just half a year ago, jaunty and jocular. It makes death a mystery to all of us as we fill our plates, almost stupidly. We, the living, eat up, walk around, talk, and occasionally glance over at the photo hanging lopsided among others on the fridge. We know that you are the same one we all just saw lying on your back in the casket, and it doesn't make sense. It would be just as easy for you to be here as not, it seems. A one-second blunder and your heart stops. It all depended on your heartbeat. That is what it boils down to. We all sense our hearts beating as we're eating. That is the difference between life and death. Such a simple thing, and life being so much bigger than just that little muscular pump. How can our existence hang on that thing. A bit of blood going in and out of arteries and veins. We are so physical it becomes disturbing. What of all our importance then if we are only a bunch of beating hearts. Some of us go right up and peer in at your picture and imagine you alive still, and that the body we buried wasn't you. But, it becomes mind games, only a pastime to deal with something we can't get to the bottom of. All of us could be lifeless in a fraction of a second. Your death makes us know that. And so, while we are still lucky enough to be alive, we eat and talk and go on beyond you with some enthusiasm. It isn't me this time, is in our manner, as we, a unit of mourners, enjoy warm life flowing through our bodies after putting your cold, stiff one away and out of sight for good.

YOUR MOTHER AND BROTHER are the only ones who avoid your photograph on the refrigerator like the plague. Your brother sees it right away and steers your mother clear of it, which then makes her know there is something she must not see, so she looks and sucks in air in a panic attack. He holds onto to her, and they wheel their way toward the food, holding back, only looking, not wanting to show any appetite, since you cannot eat. But hunger is an old familiar cue. They will join in soon enough. They will eat, survival guilt or not. They don't want to die yet. There is a lot of work to be done about your death ahead of them. It needs solving, and they will be single-minded until they figure it out. As they stand around holding their plates with everyone all the smiles and light-hearted voices. People, and these are people who know you, act as if it's okay that you are dead. They chit chat, as if it happens everyday. It's only when they come up close to your mother and father and brother that they change their tone of voice and ask the same old question, "How are you doing?" Later, your mother will say she wants to shout, "How in the Hell do you think I am doing?" And, the other common comment of, "I know, I know," she wants to curse and scream, "No, you don't know." But she just bows her head and sucks air in gasps with each new person, and buries her seething anger over the inability of people to say anything to help her.

YOUR MOTHER CROSSED OVER the street last year so she wouldn't have to run headlong into that new widow. She said, "Oh, she lost her husband. I don't want to have to say anything." That was before your death. Now she longs for someone to come up to her and say something to comfort her, even though she was one to avoid such a situation herself. She was not one to reach out to others. She would do what would make her look good according to etiquette, make the call, send the card, but then wash her hands of it. Now she has counted the phone calls, the cards, the bouquets of flowers, the curtesies, any indications of protocol paid by her friends and relatives as evidence of your worth and their concern, and has come up short of what she expected. With each phone call she groaned, as a bother and an interruption to whatever she was doing at the time, even just sitting in a chair obsessing over your death. The bell was a jangling of her nerves. She didn't want it and wanted it at the same time. She wanted to know how many people cared. And there were never enough. I wonder if she would go up to the woman who lost her husband now? Probably not. It would still be something she'd not want to give, sympathy. She'd probably still go out of her way to avoid it. There is a hardness to her mourning. No one can penetrate it with words. She stubbornly wants you back. There is no consolation in, "You'll see him again when you go there." Or, "He is in peace now." Or, "I understand your loss, We had losses, too." Nothing is appropriate. It falls on her ears and she must hold her tongue, not to mock everyone's efforts to comfort her.

ONLY ONE WOMAN impressed her. It was her hairdresser, the little Okinawan woman who has two grown sons of her own. She couldn't stop crying from the time she arrived to the time she left, and her sobs contorted not only her face but her posture. She sat round shouldered and dabbing at her dripping eyes not soon enough. Her mascara was running down her cheeks. She talked about funerals in her country. How the body is laid out for seven days in the home and everyone comes and brings food and it is a big reunion where everyone gets used to the fact of the dead one, and then they are buried. She understands why your parents wanted to have this long three-day wake. It is like the old country. And, even though the funeral director is tearing out his hair over all the people streaming in and out and having to empty the waste baskets several times a day, your parents persist with this old fashioned wake.

ONE WONDERED WHY SHE CRIED out of proportion to her relationship with you. Yes, she had cut your hair quite often when you lived here. Those silky strands you called hair. The thin, fine brown crown you let grow to cover your taxicab ears. Once you let her give you a regular man's haircut in the old style, with the sideburns and shaved short, and your students marvelled over your ears. It was a flaw they never saw before your shearing. You made fun of yourself. Took the words right out of their mouths. And the women still loved you. They seemed to overlook anything about you that might have been a fault: those ears, your income, your behavior, your habit, your age. They loved you for you, in the full sense of that senseless implication. Your way of smiling, talking, looking at them, wanting to go do things and have fun. Your Italian blood? What was it they fell in love with. Your vulnerability. The fact that you needed their help to get by?

NONE OF THEM COULD ARTICULATE what it was. All they could ever tell your mother and brother is that they "loved" you and would have done anything for you if you had asked. They longed for you to ask. But you never did. Is that what they loved. Your inaccessability? Your mother, of course, knew. She knew women loved you for what she loved you for, because you were you. She said how, when you entered the room, she just lit up like a light. She couldn't help but smile. You gave her joy. You were the joy of her life, in fact. She went that far. While Matt stood there and accepted it. He knew he was a damper on her life. He laid down the boundaries, just like your father, on what she could and couldn't do. Only you expected her to just be who she was and express it. Yet, you never encouraged her to. You went over to eat her meals. You kissed her hello and goodbye, and in between, during your visit, you laughed and talked and joked about the media on T.V., in the paper, in your experiences with your students. You made comments on everything, and she basked in all the living you were able to do up against the shut down state of your brother and father. She was glad that you wanted to stay in Australia. It was evidence that you were having a good time. At least someone in the family was enjoying life. Back on the homefront, Matt was standing guard over your mom and dad, and no one was having any fun.

HORACE HAS TO CATCH HIS PLANE back to Arizona. He wore Levis to your funeral. Maybe it was a show of disrespect because he had to pay for the dinner the night before. He flew over dressed in a suit, and appeared the two days at the funeral home to greet guests in the suit. Then the big day arrives and he's dressed like a citified cowpoke. He leaves halfway through the dinner to make it to the airport and return his rented car. Big Leroy leaves with him. He's done all he could do for your family. He's been there, standing around, eyes taking in their sadness, staying silent except for an occasional, "Man, you did all you could do," out of earshot of your parents. He came up because he knew you in Venice way back in the Eighties, and met your parents when they came down to visit. They'd drive down from Santa Barbara to see their two sons living in this artist's section of the greater L.A. area. I guess you'd clean up your act when you learned of their coming. And Matt lived with you. You had the two dogs, mother and son, old Tillie and Frankie. From Matt's marriage. Both dogs dead now. All those supplements and eventual vegetarian diets. But, so are you. This was when Matt stepped off a curb and shattered his ankle, so that he goes around now with a pin in it. The Veterans Hospital took care of everything. You never went into the Services. You were sent off to college. Matt got drafted and all he had to do to get medical expenses paid for the rest of his life was go over to Vietnam and stand around with a gun on a hilltop in the dark for two years and guard some fort until he developed an enlarged adrenal gland from fear. Yes, he shot people. He consulted a priest while there. And he was never the same after that. Never held a job either. Came home, went to college, got a degree in Health Science, and worked out of his house making catalogue orders, compiling information, selling that information to insurance companies as an independent agent. A solitary life it was, living with your parents when he moved back to Santa Barbara. Monitoring their diets and health. That's when you left California and went back to New York That's when you got beaten up and ended in the hospital buying drugs on the street. Some drug dealer made the sale and exercised his mean streak, kicking you senseless. Only Matt knew why. He lied to your parents. It would have been too painful for your mother to know how you ended up in the hospital. You'd graduated from UCLA in environmental studies, and worked for an outdoor camp taking kids into the woods upstate. That's all she knew. And she was so proud of you. But that

107

didn't last. Nothing lasted with you, Billy. You were always antsy. You wanted something else as soon as you got a job. Nothing was ever right. You should hear your brother blaming your father for that now. It was because your father terrorized that household in Longmont. He made his wife and two sons pay dearly for the security of a home in the suburbs that he offered. Did he see his responsibility as a sacrifice to his freedom and maleness perhaps? Why else would he be raging all the time? Was he as discontented as you all his life, but settled down and stayed put and worked for the same company for fifty years out of a sense of duty, and made everyone suffer for it? Why did he abuse the family he supported? He didn't seem to enjoy anything except coming home and having his wife show her appreciation by having a big meal and a perfectly kept house. Where was the joy for either of your parents, which would have trickled down to their sons? Your mother displaying only gratitude in her performance. Where was the love? Matt will dissect you father's behavior and come up with the reason you are dead. Maybe he'll be right and maybe not. There are so many variables. Remember Junior's story? His dad was a beater as well as a yeller and Junior didn't overdose. But Junior is a big brute. Matt will hold to his belief that you were tender and sensitive and lived in terror of your father's temper, however verbally expressed it was. "He never hit us once," Matt is quick to tell people.

THE PARTY IS OVER, you are buried, and everyone drifts off and leaves you and your parents standing around in Hugh and Lydia's beautiful Santa Fe decorated home. The serving dishes are empty. Everyone was full and said so. They even held their bellies and laughed. To eat at such a time baffled your family, but they ate their fill, too. And now it is time for them to go home. Home is that upstairs apartment out in that big apartment complex that is so well kept. About a thousand a month for fifteen years now. That's a mortgage on a house already. But your parents wanted money in the bank, not in a house. And both clubs are just down the street. Their new Honda will never show any wear and tear. Bright red. And only one car. You father will not let your mother out of sight. He won't buy her a car. She must schedule a ride to go have lunch with her sister Isabel every week, and to go to the hairdresser ever other week, and to go look for new curtains during the sales at other times. He keeps her under his dominance and she complies. And sighs. She sighs all the time. It is tedious being under your father's rule. She was glad you escaped. Was glad.

MATT TAKES THE WHEEL and your mother sits in the backseat, your father up front, and they make their way down the hill and to their life in the apartment which they claim is too small. The hard work is now beginning. The people have gone, all respects and sympathies paid, flowers and cards and fruit baskets delivered, and they are alone. As they climb the stairs the phone is ringing. Matt grabs the key from your father and opens the door, grabs the phone. It is your father's sister. Eighty-five years old in N.Y. She wants to know if Matt is doing drugs, too. Your father goes into the bedroom to talk to her. He comes out shaking his head. She is a blunt woman, much like he is. Their father was blunt. He badgered his family with the same yelling and controlling.

HIS WIFE PUT ON THREE HUNDRED POUNDS and never left the house for the last twenty years of her life. She may as well have been chained to the kitchen sink. He, your grandfather, did all the shopping. She was a "fabulous cook," according to your dad. He remembers his mother's eight-course meals every night for all of her married life. And the old man made his own wine, kept a vegetable garden right there in the middle of the city. Went out everyday and poured tar in the streets for a living. Worked and sweat, came home, yelled and screamed, ate and slept, cultivated his garden and died, leaving his home to his son, your dad. That's how your dad escaped the city and moved his family out to the suburbs. His own dad never learned to read or write in either language, Italian or English. He was from Sicily. A hard working, hard living man. And thin. He lived long. He never questioned whether he lived right. He knew he did everything a man was suppose to do. He did what his father did. He supported a wife, son and two daughters in some respectability. He taught his son to get out and work early. Your dad only went to sixth grade and made a good living. He made a better living than some educated men, and didn't hesitate to point that out when he could. Work used to be the most honorable thing in America. Not education. A man worked. Your father wasn't prepared for two sons who didn't work. Sons who had time to do nothing and drift through life, and now, get in trouble and

110

finally die. After your death, your father punched his fist into his hand and cursed the fact that you never got a real job. He said he never wanted to hear the word "yoga" again. It was the life of a dilettante. You were always trying to find yourself. He didn't even know what that meant. "Find yourself, what the hell is that. You know who you are when you work. That's who you are." He pointed his thumb to his wife once, when asked who his boys took after. With furrowed eyebrows, he frowned. He never got a son. Not the kind he thought he'd have. One he could play ball with. He got a couple of sissies. Ninnies. They stuck close to their mother, and still padded around her livingroom in their stockinged feet at forty-three and forty-eight, as if they were adolescents. Their bodies were smooth and soft as daughters. Hair perfumed, skin emolliented. Clothes immaculately pressed and clean. No sweat stains under the arms or around the collars. No calluses on their palms. Two college graduation diplomas in frames on the wall. And for what. All that money spent to learn what? Yet he was proud of those diplomas for whatever they meant. Matt said that he never heard a word about going to college from his parents during his whole childhood. And he could have gotten a baseball scholarship. You two boys excelled in sports. Matt in baseball, and you in football. That was the direction your parents guided you. Even today, the four of you sat on the couch and rooted for your teams together. Your mother was in their shouting with the three of you. She knew all the player and the scores. It was what your family did together. That was the way you communicated.

YOU CAN SEE THEM NOW. There they are without you, changing channels and finding out the scores. Which team, which players, how close, how good the plays themselves. They have nothing to say about your death now. They distract themselves with the sports channel, and then your father goes in and watches his programs on the color T.V. in the big bedroom, and Matt goes in and watches his on the little black and white, and leave your mother to the big console T.V. in the Iivingroom, where she nods off, afraid to turn off the television to be alone with your death.

THEIR WORK IS JUST BEGINNING. Now that you are buried, and everyone has gone home, the phone has stopped ringing, flowers and cards no longer coming, they have to face each other.

THE BLAME BEGINS. You father gets up and goes to your grave the next morning and sits and has a long session with you. You are the only one who knows what he says. Matt can imagine that he pounds the ground with his fist and curses you in one breath, and cries like a baby and tells you how much he loved you in the other. He, no doubt preaches the work ethic, and raises his hard-worked hand to the skies and asks the question, why? Why did it happen to him, a son who went into yoga and meditation and all that crap that led to drugs. Those kind of people sitting around smoking pot trying to find themselves instead of getting jobs and being responsible. How could it happen to him? And, he may ask, under his breath, "Did you think I was too hard on you? That's what your brother says. He's blaming me now, for this. He thinks I killed you. Tell me. Give me a sign. I worked all my life. This is what I get? Oh, I should have put down my foot. I don't know...." And what else. What does he say to you Billy? Are you sorry now. Do you wish you'd listened to your dad and brother. Are you somewhere knowing "the truth" now? Or, like the Hindu religion you half-believed in, are you reincarnated as some lower form of life to give you another chance to do it right and come back higher and higher until you reach perfection? You certainly weren't ready for Nirvana, that highest state of being. Are you a dog? That's what someone said. That you were afraid you'd come back as a dog because of the way you treated Frankie. You felt you didn't do something right or he wouldn't have died. And you not being there when he died played on your conscience, so you felt you must live a dog's life to understand what he went through. Your father rolled his eyes over that one. A dog was suppose to die. He was eight years old. Yes, you starved him by making him eat vegetables, but not out of cruelty, only stupidity. You can be forgiven for that. Your heart meant well, it was all the ideas you had of the evils of eating flesh that led you astray concerning your dog. You didn't have any basis in reality in some things. Your father was all common sense, and you were none. That's what baffled him. He never understood how you could believe that nonsense you studied. It may be true for Indians, but Americans, and especially Italians, he'd throw up his hands and shake his head.

YOUR MOTHER HAS STOPPED GOING to the gym. She refuses to keep her body fit. Why should she make that effort to do aerobics if your are rotting in the ground. She sits and sniffles. She has gotten soft. Her arms hang like the curtains on the kitchen window. Her belly bloats, and hips have widened. She just sits. Your death has given her and your brother permission to do what they like to do best: sit and watch T.V. They have no guilt. They watch the tube all day long, falling asleep while the sun is blazing outside, still in their house coat and pajamas. Your father comes in flushed from his exercises glowering at those two. He doesn't know what to do. They won't budge from the soft safety of the padded apartment. And there is nothing brewing in the kitchen. You mother used to have his breakfast ready when he came in. Now the kitchen is cold, and he must go stand in the little archway and stare at the stove, to get her to get up and try to make a little something for him. She doesn't want to eat herself and neither does Matt. It is what he feared, her grief has separated her from him and he can't reach her. He has no more control over her. Even, passive, she resists him in a way she couldn't before. She did her duties by him before. But now that he has killed you, she refuses to serve him, and begins to confess to Matt behind his back that she never liked your father much. Once married to him, she stayed, but when she discovered he was abusive, she clammed up, stopped having sex with him, and made the best of it. She is sorry now that she "provided such a father" for her sons. Matt is dumbfounded by this gush of honesty from your mother. It is a first. She has never let him in on any of her feeling

114

about anything yet. Maybe the media, but never her personal life. How she felt about your father was a mystery to him. How she felt about being the last of the American housewives, subservient to a dominant male was a mystery. He, as a male, assumed she liked her role. That it afforded her the security she wanted, and sacrificing her "freedom" was a price she wanted to pay. He, himself, couldn't conceive of his mother "free" anyway. It would have been as much of a threat to him as to your father. The three of you males kept her in her place. She didn't have a chance. Too bad she didn't have a daughter.

YOUR MOTHER PROTESTS in the Sixties' way, demonstrating her disapproval, without knowing it is what your generation did. She is having a sit out and a starvation to avenge your death and bring down the old white male tradition that has wronged women and lesser men, all children and animals and you. There is no stopping her now. Your father even fears her power. He keeps his distance, his blue eyes leveled on her, watchful. What will she do next. She may even take the car and go off without his knowing where. It would be a first. He is no longer sure of her behavior. She has broken their pact to be obedient. She acts in the Gandhian civil disobedience manner, for a greater cause. She has joined you in India, in this way. But, of course, it is all unspoken and subconscious. She does not define her new behavior. She just is it. As your brother Matt is always saying, "You live in the moment in your isness." She has transcended the daily toil under the man, and knows in her heart that it is right to do so. Following her husband's orders has come to a stop. She is a true Feminist, listening to her needs, no longer putting herself aside. You are still teaching, your mother a student.

MATT SETS UP A HOSPICE counseling session. They both go in and talk to a lanky man with the name of Pugh. The whole thing stinks, alright. This business of exposing their feelings. It is new to both of them. They've spent their lives keeping quiet, now they must talk. They don't know where to begin, what to say. This is outside what they know. How do you have a session with a counselor. What are the rules to follow. They look for structure and guidance. They spend an hour and a half talking as he directs them with questions and statements of fact as they speak. He sees that they are novices in self-discovery. They cry, unexpectedly and try to cover it, embarrassed expressing emotion. He tells them there are no rules here. He emphasizes that whatever they do is what they do. After the session, Matt quotes this over and over, with wonderment. The guidelines are whatever they have inside them to tell and feel. He watches your mother, and she glances at him from time to time. Mostly she is his subject and he, her audience. He is still taken up with protocol. A mother is made a certain way so that her child's death is something she can't take. it is an assumption he comes to discover he has. And he holds your mother to it without words. He approves of the dark gloom, knowing that she cannot be any other way. He may even expect her to die over your death. It seems appropriate. How can a mother simply grieve and get over it. It's inconceivable. He is a thinking man, and this is what his thinking tells

116

him. Where does he get his information, though. Is it only his male role conjuring these images of what a mother is suppose to do upon the death of her son. If she donned a red dress and went out dancing, would he be the first to snatch her back into the house and make her change and insist she sit in her upholstered chaise with the lever to elevate her old feet, and stay in the mourning mode? Would the ability to get over your death be a threat to his image of her. He so believes in her motherly qualities, which he sees as frail, that he insists she go according to code.

EME ATTACKS HIM ON THIS. She listens to the report on the Hospice session, and gets wind of his definition of your mother "not being able to take your death." She wants to know what he means by this. When he can't explain what he means, she insists it's his need to put your mother in this position. He feels assaulted. She goes on about his faulty view of mothers. Mothers are tough. They can take the death of a child as is evident down through history. What about the trail of infant and child deaths all across America as the Pioneers came out West. What about all the war torn countries. She accuses him of not wanting to believe a mother is that tough. That it scares him, because he has his mind made up, and is afraid to have to adjust it. Who would he be without all his beliefs in the way things "should" be. "Have to be." That his mental structure is based on his own emotional frailty, not his mother's. He leaves her presence. He calls her a savage. Ruthless. Brutal. That she is like those South American hunters with the blow darts that inflict death as they strike, with their poisoned tips. That her words hurt, and he must go lick his wounds. He goes back to your mother, and studies her. Could it be that she is, indeed, going to get through this alive, and someday be able to chit chat as if it is just part of her conversation, that "before Billy died," or "After Billy's death....bla, bla," and not have it move her to tears? The thought is an abomination of your memory at this point. Eme calls up and persists, "What does "not take it" mean?" She insists that Matt explain what he means by that overused phrase. "How does one "not take" something?" He is silent.

MATT WILL UNDERGO A CHANGE in his self-concept. He will find out that he, too, can take it. He won't want to believe that either. How hard is he. The counselor will tell him that was one of the "survival guilts" the Holocaust victims who lived had to deal with. They questioned why others died and they lived. What was it in them that was tough enough to survive. A certain selfishness, hard-heartedness. They admired the relatives who were too sensitive and delicate take such an atrocity, and lived with doubt about their own sensibilities after that. Matt will confess to Eme (who goes back to her time and again, knowing she will not mince her words, counting on her ingenuous bent) and tell her that it occurs to him that he has something to get up in the morning for, now, whereas before, he didn't. Now Matt has a direction, a goal, purpose. Obsessing over your death is a project he whole-heartedly embraces. Now he knows what his own life is about—your death. He was born to know this and go into it in depth, and find out all about it. He is almost relieved from the doldrums of having nothing real to do, but bide time and sell a little health information from time to time, maybe twice a month. The rest of his time was spent corralling Eme, keeping track of her the way your father did your mother. The territoriality instinct a full time occupation.

KEEPING YOU ALIVE KNIT YOUR FAMILY together. They will learn through counselling that the sibling who "acts out" is the one who is trying to save the family system by diverting attention onto himself so as to bring the parents together. Well, you certainly accomplished that. Your mother and father spent many evenings watching you thrash around in that twin bed in withdrawals. They couldn't fight between themselves as long as they were worried over you. Now they don't know who they are. Like Kissinger lost his position in the world politics when Communism ended, or had to refocus sheepishly over his sudden unimportance, your brother and mother and father now flounder for that focal point they had under the old family system. Their every waking moment had been your well-being. The three of them bumbling around in that apartment in their ritualistic living wondering how you were, calling, finding out, telling you to knock it off, or praising you for being "good' kept them from each other's throats.

BUT THEY FAILED, DIDN'T THEY. Their goal was to keep you alive, and they didn't do it. Matt feels your parents' disapproval. He had posed as the big important good son who did everything right, including monitoring your behavior. Now he feels your mother's disappointment and your father's scorn. He pranced and strutted his better education, his workshops in how to deal with a loved one who is using, and your mother trusted he knew what he was doing. Your father never thought it was worth a damn, and now he knows he was right. Matt pushed his old fashioned ideas aside and chastised him for his style, yelling and badgering, and promoted himself as the new intelligent way to handle the situation. The male competition is nasty. Your father tries to hold his tongue, but has never been successful. He is his father's son. He belittles your brother's ways. Matt fights back in a way he never thought he could. He blames your parents, both of them, for not cooperating with him and going to drug counseling and finding out how to handle you. They are a pack of dogs. Matt is not about to take all the blame, even if he had wanted all the credit for as long as you were kept alive. He sacrificed for you. He put his own life on hold to be the family caretaker, and now they're turning on him. The sportmanship is to hit below the belt. After all the games they watched. Matt is a poor loser. He is angry. His counselor therapist tells him to punch pillows when he finds himself alone at home. He calls Eme and tells her that he always felt that it was unfair to be singled out to be the one to see to your care. He was tired of that role, but caught in it. There was no way out. He felt the pressure for his whole life. Your health and safety came before even his wife, however brief that marriage was. He had to report your well-being to your parents and assure them so they would not worry. He shouldered the whole brunt of your addiction and never complained until now. Now that he's failed to do the superhuman feat he wants them to accept their part of the blame. He even attacks your mother by asking her why she refused to go with him to those workshops at the Rehab Center. She hollers that she doesn't know. She is hurt that Matt wants her to not only grieve but to regret her own treatment of you. All she did was love you. And now she was in error. She did not arm herself properly to deal with your drug habit.

THE QUESTION OF THE VALIDITY of the contents of the envelope that was put into your casket, surfaces. Your mother has asked why that woman would write such a note if there was no truth to it. Does Billy have a child somewhere, as it said? Matt confides in Eme over the phone. He called her the night of the funeral and tells her that you did father a son back in 1987 in Venice, California. The girl went ahead and had your baby and you didn't want to have anything to do with it. It was in the height of the Hippie movement. You were practicing Yoga on the beach. This pretty little girl of 18 came along and liked you. She sat in the sand, took the Lotus position as much as her flexibility would allow, and let you instruct her on the value of deep breathing and meditation. Later you went to bed and had sex. You fell in love. She went off the pill at your request. It was three months into the relationship and you were sure you were in love forever and ever. You wanted to have a baby. She wanted to have your baby. You were working at a beach cafe. She'd come and give you the latest report on her pregnancy test. In those days there were no at-home chemical tests sold at the pharmacy. Women had to wait until they missed a period and then the doctor could take a blood test and affirm that she was pregnant. You received the news in that three-month period. You continued to be lovers for a couple of months, and then you got cold feet. and decided she should get an abortion. There were no legal abortions in those days, but women knew where to go. You got nasty. You stopped seeing her. She was a beautiful little girl, long and thin with a Miss America face. There are photos from back then that your family will soon see. A beautiful boy was born. He looked just like you. She threatened you with a paternity suit. She was on Welfare, and being a single mother was going to be a hardship. And, besides, it was your idea in the first place. You planned it with her, talked her into it. And then bailed out. The unfairness of it got to her. She came to your cafe to show you the baby before all the nastiness started, hoping you would not be able to resist being the father of such an infant. You went along for nine months, even visiting her at her parent's house, and giving her a twenty dollar bill, and going to Sears and buying the baby a little coat. And then you didn't want her in your life anymore. That's when she said she'd get a lawyer. You got mean and said you'd go to court with all your friends and they'd testify that they'd all slept with her, and get off that way. She was hurt and angry, but she loved her baby and went home, still drawing a Welfare check, and made the best of it. There are albums full of the good job she did. Your parents will cry over them in the not too distant future.

EME INSISTS MATT TELL YOUR MOTHER that it is true. You do have a son and he's 17 years old and has been looking for you for the last three years. Matt says he doesn't think your mother can take the news. Eme says she will tell if he doesn't. That it has been a crime to keep a grandchild from a couple who have longed for one for all these years. Now, at 79 and 80, they can at least have that, and especially if he looks like you. It is as if you live. You are alive through this grandson. That he must not wait one more minute to break the good news to them. Matt has known for 17 years. He has kept your secret. There is a lot at stake in telling now, at this late date. They could be mad at him or they could "not be able to take it." You mother had said aloud that day in the funeral home that she wished she'd never read that note to you. Eme says, "Tell her now and call me back."

MATT CALLS BACK. He has told your mother. She is joyous tinged with anguish. She cries. All those years gone. Then she takes hope. Eme accosts Matt, "See, it was an act of cruelty to keep it from her. How could you watch your parents grow old, knowing they wanted a grandchild, knowing they had one, and not tell?" Matt has no answer except that he didn't know how they would take it and that you would not want him to divulge your past. Your family kept things from each other. It was their way. Matt will learn a thing or two about your parents before all this is over, although it will never be over. Your death, and now the life you left behind will crack your family open like a rotten gourd. if you're watching, Billy and have those special powers attributed to the dead, you will

123

know what's inside your mother's head. Now you see she is worrried about your father's reaction to the news. She warns Matt not to tell him, warning him beyond need that he is unpredictable, as if Matt doesn't know this. This is just one of many secrets they have kept from your predictably volatile father. The two of them still fear his response after a lifetime with him, and move about under the same roof with the knowledge between them looking over at your father in all his innocence. Is it a kind of power they like to have over him. Their way of fighting back. The passive aggression counselors talk about? They know, he doesn't.

AGAIN, MATT CONSULTS EME, whose expertise as a psychotherapist he regards with respect. She worked as an MFCC intern for two agencies for seven years and then gave it up. That was five years ago. She, again encourages "the truth will out," approach. "To make the mind whole," she chides, since Matt has gone on about "holistic" living as his philosophy/religion/science. So Matt takes his father out to get coffee with the plan to go out to Eme's just in case he goes into a rage or falls apart. Matt is afraid of emotion. Your mother's tears scare him, as if he is a little boy. And Matt is afraid to be alone with your father when he shows his feeling over your son. He wants Eme to be a buffer, believing your father will behave in front of her. That he is a macho man and won't want to expose his innards to a woman, even if he respects her judgment.

ON THE RIDE OUT TO EME'S, with the paper cups of coffee burning your father's hands and about to spill as he balances the bag of muffins between his feet, Matt tells your father that he has a grandson 17 years old. They arrive just in time with the take-outs from Our Daily Bread steaming and sending out a nice aroma. Eme puts the treats on a picnic table. Your father walks long-armed and short-legged rendered a primate who's just been alerted to a new occurrence in the jungle. His body wired with energy and cranium weighted with knowledge. His brow furrows, mouth sets, and he begins opening the lids off the coffee cups, and bags of muffins with distraction, almost spilling everything. He sits heavy in a slouch and shakes his head back and forth, glaring out with those blue eyes like he'd like to get someone by the neck and knuckle them down. He's been known to say to anyone crossing him in the past, "In New York we mop the street with someone like you."

OUTSIDE, AT THE PATIO TABLE, with the early spring sunshine anointing him with gold, your father is silent, contemplating it. Eme sits across from him and waits for him to talk about the news. He doesn't say anything and looks in his lap. You knew this trait of the pseudo pout as his demonstrative style, didn't you. He knows all eyes are on him. As he puts on his show of silence, Matt mills in the background, not sitting down. He doesn't approve of your father drinking coffee and won't be a part of the ritual nor will he put himself too close to your father's accusatory nature at this point; but he eyes the muffins from a distance. Your father begins to react. He shakes his full head of startlingly white hair back and forth meditatively. The wheels are turning inside. This is a once in a lifetime kind of thing, and "whatcha gonna do?" is his demeanor. He finally gruffs out a few brief words, "Imagine. A thing like that." And that releases Eme's tongue. She gushes all the words your family will not say. She tells your dad how wonderful it is that he has a grandson. That you live through him. That he looks just like you the woman said. That you live. "Billy lives!" She is excited, hoping to ignite some exuberance in your father. He blurts out in an agonized tone, "All I ever wanted in this world was a daughter-in-law and a grandson. I could have played ball with him." And he lays his head on his arms across the table and sobs, high and loud. And then looks up, his face red and wet, eyes full and running over with tears. He says, "I wish she would have put him in jail. She should have made him do the right thing. He got out of his responsibility. That son of a bitch. She should have called the cops. He didn't want to support the kid, and so we lost out...." Absent of feeling, he adds, "There will have to be a blood test, of course." And then sits there stunned and stubborn. He doesn't want to be made a fool, meeting a grandchild that isn't even his. Eme looks at Matt. How could he request proof? is in her glance. She will later say, "Now I see where Billy got it."

YOU ARE BEYOND YOUR FATHER'S REACH or he'd come after you. He'd really have some dealing power over you now with this information. But you escaped. He sits in a stupor and sips at his coffee, tears a piece off a muffin absently, and pokes it in his

126

mouth and chews as if it's tasteless. Matt takes his cue and comes in and takes up a muffin and begins eating it as if he is starving to death. Food has become a punishment to Matt. The equation in his head is: If Billy is dead, who has a right to eat—so that when he gets a morsel in his hand he devours it as any ravenous animal would.

YOUR BROTHER AND FATHER LEAVE Eme's place as quickly as they arrived. They accomplished what they wanted, and now they will call and find out when they can see the kid. Matt calls Eme that night and asks if she will drive down to Dana Point with them, next week. They will book two rooms and meet the boy and visit for three days. She agrees. In fact, she wouldn't miss it for the world. Meanwhile your mother and brother pass the time fixed to the T.V. The O.J. trials blares on. His team of black lawyers vs. one white woman and one black man. They watch it day and night. The commentary comes on at nine P.M., and sends them off to bed with murder in their head. Eme tells your brother that it isn't good for your mother to be dwelling on this gruesome subject when she is mourning you. But there is no tearing them from the screen.

THE DRIVE DOWN TO DANA POINT has arrived. A lot of fuss to pack the car, have it serviced, make reservations, and leave at the appointed time to get there at the right hour to meet the boy is made. Between your mother, Matt, and your father, you can imagine the "labor intensive" effort they put into this out of the ordinary appointment. Matt thinks in terms of energy expended in any endeavor, and tries to keep your parents at a minimum, as you remember. That doesn't mean he has thought through the value of high energy vs. low energy. It is one more of his spiritual Eastern religious assumptions of being calm and serene as the highest human state. But, you know your family. The smallest detail will require maximum attention. Your mother will be exhausted by the time she gets into the car. She will be clutching a bagful of something for the trip. You father will be strutting out, sighing over the tediousness of preparing for a hundred and fifty mile motor trip. He likes his home; he never took his family on a weekend adventure all through your childhood. And your mother and you were ready to go anytime. A whole lifetime waiting to go somewhere, and finally she gets to. Matt balks over the bother of it all. Your parents are too old, he believes, for new experiences. He wishes to keep their brain in fibrillation. And this trip will enter into the realm of feelings. The fact that they must feel something for your son has thrown him into upset. He is worried over their well-being. No wonder he never told them before he was forced to. And they blame him for the delay? He knew it would cause all this turmoil, complaining over the ordeal of getting ready, driving that far, and wondering what the outcome will be when they get there. The unknown quality has them all in a dither. There is not an ounce of spontaneity in their spirit as they do their duty by this new grandson. If they could be forced to admit it, they may all say they are sorry they ever found out. But, that would be disgraceful, so they trudge on. You father snaps the trunk shut with certainty. The motel cocktail hour all neatly packed in plastic bags and tupperware. Tupperware your mother reads by size, "Give me a number 2 lid for this container," she instructed Matt, who bent down and crouched to find the impeccably stored set on the bottom shelf. Or, "I need a number six for the hummus."

MATT TAKES HIS POSITION behind the wheel, adjusts the seat, rolls down the window, adjusts the rearview mirrors, puts on his seatbelt, turns to see if your parents are strapped in, and then puts the car in reverse, and ever so slowly, backs out of the carport, and goes in the opposite direction. He always takes the longer route to the freeway, which he thinks is faster in the long run. The passenger seat is empty. They will stop and pick Eme up on the way. Matt drives. He is the only son now. He turns on the O.J. Simpson trial. Rosa Lopez is in her third day of testimony, a testimony which contradicts itself each day. One day she cannot walk the dog in the ivy where it would give her a perfect view of seeing the white Bronco, and the next she is knee-deep with snakes and rats that live in the ivy. She grows increasingly well-dressed and groomed with each day and calls her beloved benefactor, the defense lawyer, "Mr. Johnny." These are the details of the trial your mother wanted to laugh with you over. After Eme is picked up and strapped in beside Matt, she turns and makes faces over every lie Rosa Lopez tells. And then static sets in, and Matt is desperate to find the coverage on another station. He curses the long ride without the distraction of the trial. Your family does not want to be left with all this time and close proximity and pass it without the media as their means of communication. Matt punches the car radio off, and hits the steering wheel with frustration. How will your mother ever survive her grief without the trial to put her mind to. He glances over his shoulder to see if she is taking the disappointment okay. She begins to sniffle into her tissue. Eme reaches back and touches her shoulder to Matt's cue. He has given a toss of his head, ever so slightly, and a dart of his eyes. His dilemma is that he must keep both hands on the wheel and his eyes on the road. It is Eme's job to physically console your mother now. Your father has no patience with her tears. His great work hands are folded in his lap. He will have none of this reaching over and consoling a woman who won't stop bawling no matter what he does. She is out of his hands. It is out of his hands. He can't solve this for her. He just sits like a lump and has to let it happen to him, too. He hunches and bites down on his old mouth, giving her a sidelong glower from time to time.

THEY MAKE GOOD TIME. They pass through the Los Angeles area without slowing down on the 405. They are there before they thought they would be. The area where the boy lives with his mother and half sister is a resort community. Nicole Simpson's family live here, too. In fact, they will discover that Nicole will be the new last name taken by the boy's mother for no reason at all except she liked it and didn't want her old married name anymore. Matt pulls over to use the phone and let your parents use the restroom. Your mother is saying, "I hope they like us. What if they don't like us."

EME ASSURES HER that they wouldn't have invited them down if that was their attitude. Your mother remains silent, holding onto her tissue, clutching her own ribcage. She has taken to wearing dark glasses since your death. No one can see her eyes, so cannot tell if she is okay or not. Matt uses his ears, not his eyes to detect her anguish. He comes out of the phone booth with his usual business manner. He has made the call, gotten the last minute directions, and they will be waiting. This is the countdown. Your father gets back into the car and is hauled around like so much luggage. All that he's ever learned and known is useless to him at this point. He says, "I never thought a thing like this would happen to me. To our family. Imagine." And then sits, only baggage.

MATT COULD BE A TAXI DRIVER for the ease with which he finds the address. There're your parents, peering out the car widows looking at the entrance to the neighborhood, the guard at the gate, and finally the street and the house. A very nice place. Expensive. Palms trees decorating the front entrance, a hired gardener, landscape, wide sidewalks, and there's the number. That's the house where their grandson lives. Matt parks the car. Your mother begins to whimper. Your father begins to unhook the seatbelts, his and his wife's. They climb out of the backseat, Matt and Eme out of the front, and they hand Eme the family camera. "Here, dear, get some pictures," your mother tells her, as they dust at their trousers and skirt, and run a hand over their hair, standing there at the curb. And then there he is. Your son. He is coming out the front door straight toward them. He's a big guy. A galoot of sorts. Bigger than you. Like a Paul Bunyan version of you. Neither fish nor fowl at his age. His feet bigger than the rest of him, and the rest of him over-sized. He has pimples and two earrings in each ear up high in the cartilage, not the lobe. His coloring is good, tan, rosy. He's got the blush of youth on the jaw line where teenage boys blush. And his eyes are dark but bright. He's a cute kid who dwarfs your parents. He goes for your mother first addressing her as "Grandma." He tries to turn to your dad, but your mother is crushed against his chest, sobbing and saying she is so sorry. "Oh, I'm so sorry," over and over. He's a nice guy. His arms are all the way around her and he is bent down to hold her in real affection. She finally pulls her head back from his big flannel plaid chest and takes a look at his face, patting his clean shaven cheek. She is clearly in pain. He looks like you. His smile, jumping up in the corners is exactly like yours. His bright naughty eyes, the expression he keeps, a certain composure he had, and warmth. It's all there. Your father is waiting his turn. Your mother is the star today. So your father gazes up at this new occurrence in his life as if it is truely an apparition. As if he suddenly just appeared out of nowhere, which is exactly what has happened. One day he wasn't anybody's grandfather, and now he has a full-blown grandson. As the boy, staying bent, grasps your old

132

dad, there are the painful sobs of an old man. All your mother has to do is love. But your father, well, men are more complicated. It is not as easy being a grandfather. He could have played ball with the kid all these years. He could have gone around with him. He could have known him. He could have bragged down at the club about him. He could have carried photographs of him in his wallet. And now here he is. What's a guy gonna do. How do you just step into a big boy's life and start being a grandfather.

IT TAKES YOUR FATHER A SPLIT SECOND to find out it comes to him naturally. If you're watching from up above or that other realm, you see that your dad stays true to form. First off, his gruff remarks. "You're a big guy. What'aya? 185?" The kid grins. It breaks your mother's heart. It's your grin. He shakes Matt's hand, who offers it with a kind of distant formality. He shows no affection whatsoever. This is all duty to your brother. What good is your kid when you aren't here, is in his manner. The mother comes down the walk. She's waited, given it enough time for her son to have center stage and now she appears on long stems in black tights, a t-shirt, and with lots of mussy long brown hair. Her legs, slender as a model's, going all the way up to wide hip bones. She walks as if she is on the ramp. As pretty as Miss America. The blue eyes, the pretty mouth, the perfect oval face and nose. A Hollywood type to be sure. It turns out she is a personal trainer, has her own gym right here in the house, and will have to keep an appointment in two hours with one of her clients. At almost forty, she has the presence of a girl. She is still the little eighteen-year-old you got pregnant in Venice, California back in 1978. She was a beauty then, and still is. How tall were you, Billy? She looks like she would tower over you the way she does your little family. She's perched on those stilts that seem twice as long as yours, but when asked in later conversation, she tells us you were the same height. And like you, she keeps slim and fit. Later we will hear her say that she has killer abs. You two still had a lot in common. You could compare your muscles and talk nutrition all night long, and laugh about how innocent you were back then, and not even be aware that you hadn't outgrown anything. You'd still be butting heads and competing for the limelight. Both of you were primadonnas. It's evident now, after meeting her. But, while everyone is still going through the formalities of greeting, she keeps a regal poise.

THIS IS THE LOFTIEST the visiting will ever be, this introductory phase, which puts everyone on their best behavior and causes them to reach toward their higher minds and away from the everyday common thinking. It is something out of the ordinary, after all, this subject of having made life and never acknowledged it way back then. Later, everyone but your mother will be eager to show their seedy side. Darla, the kid's mother, will use her California slang phrases soon enough. And she will go off into the new spiritualism of the day. All the goddess talk, and the guidance she gets by listening to her "true" self, whatever that might be. It's all in her self-esteem workshop handbooks. Your parents will remain without comment. In the course of the meeting, she will expose herself as the little hippie girl of old, who didn't bother to go to college, but married a rich lawyer and led the life of a consumer, spending heavily for the past seventeen years, who took a shortcut to education by adopting the pop culture as her medium, and living in the world of innunendo, as if she's gone into the depths of subjects and it's only the tip of the iceberg she speaks from.

SHE LEADS YOUR BEWILDERED FAMILY into her house. She is moving to Sacramento. The over-sized furniture from her big house in Beverly Hills, is sitting around facing the wrong direction waiting for the movers. She has explained all this to Matt over the phone. They are moving to the Sacramento Valley near a lake, the day after tomorrow because that's where her new boyfriend got a job. He's a paramedic now, but was a fireman until he got his ear knocked off by a fire hose. She is madly in love with him. She confesses that she married the lawyer just for his money as a single mother back then in Venice. She went to a lawyer to sue you for paternity, and he ended up marrying her. He had two sons of his own and a bitter ex-wife. She was impressed by seeing his name on a big shiny office building in the heart of Beverly Hills. As he courted her, she learned that he had been forced to marry some J.A.P. to please his wealthy mother. And he spent a miserable decade with the woman. When he saw Darla walk in to get legal advice, with your darling infant on her hip, and wearing her hippy gauze madras and feathers and beads, and needing financial support, it was love at first sight. He had the finances to dazzle her

135

with, and proceeded to get rid of the first wife, take his two small sons, avoid his mother's caustic tongue, and bring in the new bride, Darla and son. He did your job, Billy. He raised your son for thirteen years. Then, all hell broke loose.

YOUR SON, MAYNARD, THEY NAMED HIM, had adolescent growing pains. He was tired of being razzed by his stepbrothers about where his dad was, beat them both up, took to going out and drinking and taking drugs. He ended up being sent to a private school for such "bad" boys up north. A very expensive school that would straighten him out with the Twelve Step Program principles as the basis. Instead of religion, instead of education, again the new psychology/spiritualism combo, to give him some answers and empowerment. Why does shit happen? Because your vibes are off in the universe kind of belief. The kid swallowed it hook, line, and sinker. And came out thinking like his mother. Now, together, they can talk the same line, using the same vocabulary, and grin at each other as if they have the key to life and happiness and the universe, while everyone else is still floundering. Darla will top off the visit with how God answers her prayers. The rich lawyer was giving her a hard time about child custody and spousal support, when he had a stroke. Now he quivers in a chair somewhere and can't even speak or sign a document. And it was right after the adoption papers came through, so her son is an heir to the fortune. She said she was cursing him, and raising her fist to the sky, and saying she wished he'd die, when she got the good news that he all but died. She laughed and called it "instant karma" for him, saying, "what goes around, comes around," and every other cliché she could think of. Your parents sat, as if in a bad movie, silent, uncomfortable.

AND SO ENDED THE FIRST VISIT. Everyone was exhausted by the unexpressed emotions. There was a strain holding back all that the eye could see and the mouth couldn't say. And not expressing what was in the heart. The kid sat at the piano and pounded out a self-composed piece which was mostly noisy, and then played the theme from The Godfather. Everyone laughed. He so wanted to be Italian, his mother explained to your parents and to Matt who sat without cracking a smile the whole time. He guarded your mother and father, herding them with his eyes like a loyal dog. Your mother cried when she heard the piano playing. You were musical, too. And they told him about your guitar under their bed that they would give to him. They also took out a gift and handed it to him. He carefully cramped his size and crouched at the coffee table opening the tissue paper, and saw the twisted vines within. It was a circle used by the Indians as a sign of unity and wholeness. They used it in their religious ceremonies. He knew what it was exactly, and breathed out a breath of wonder. He had learned to make these things up in his private school a few years ago. He held it up and gazed at it to display his reverence for his father's possession. He swore he would cherish it.

DARLA HAD ASKED MATT what they liked to snack on during the visit and she got an answer she apparently didn't like. She served nothing at all. He told them later that when she told him she'd have a few snacks, and he suggested rice crackers and non-fat cheese, fruit, and maybe decaffinated coffee, she gave the equivalent of a nod of the head over the phone. Nothing was offered. Matt said nothing. He was insulted.

EVERYONE BID EVERYONE GOODBYE until dinnertime, and Matt drove your parents and Eme over to the hotel. It was a hundred and fifty dollars a night for two rooms. The smallest Holiday Inn in the world, across from the beach, and beautifully kept. "Only 15 units," Matt explained. Your parents had what looked like a bridal room with a white organdy canopy above the head of the bed. Your father kept joking that they were just married. No one laughed. Your mother never even let the words touch her ears. She acted as if he hadn't spoke at all and went about preparing the wine and cheeses they'd brought down from home. Matt and Eme went into their room and flopped down on the two double beds. Matt flipped on the television, and got commentaries about the trial. Eme got into a hot shower and crawled under the covers for a nap. She never forgot that she was not family, and that none of this really mattered to her, even though she and Matt had been seeing each other for five years. Even though she did know you and took a few of your classes. Even though she did accept dinner invitations on a Sunday once in awhile over the years. Even though she pretended it mattered. Even though she felt like a hypocrite. Even though..... She slept on the clean slick sheets and wished your brother was a ravenous lover, that he wasn't consumed with your death, and before that, with your pending death.

THE PLAN WAS TO MEET at Emilios for dinner. It is a big popular restaurant right on the harbor. All there is to do at Dana Point is to eat out and shop. The town is built brand new and all at once on dry barren rolling hills alongside the ocean. Nothing but low brush and wild grasses grew before the developers got ahold of it. A Southern California climate just above the Mexican border about sixty miles. Someone got the bright idea to build estates, and then shopping malls went in to accomodate the new and monied population. A spot on the map between Los Angeles and San Diego. A getaway place for city workers to flee to and hide in expensive housing. No trees had to be cut. No mountains shovelled level. The dullest of landscapes made pretty now by the bright lights of fast food places, boutiques, and motels, and good restaurants. Darla and her crew arrive in her big new van with curtains in the windows, seats upholstered in velvet and lined up in rows like a bus. She maneuvers to a parking place and finds your parents and Matt and Eme waiting to be seated. Her mother has joined them. She a woman in her sixties, grey and slim from cigarets and coffee. The kind of slimness that comes from hyperactivity, not health. She was a waitress/manager with her husband, Darla's father for thirty years. He still has the restaurant, but is married to a 22-year-old waitress who looks like a young version of the wife. Slim, blonde, plain. She will get into her stories about their marriage only when asked by Eme, who feels free to ask personal questions out of sheer curiosity, not considering the appropriateness of it or not. She is an outsider and simply wants to know why the man divorced and married one of his young waitresses. The mother tells her that he had always said he wanted to have a 22-year-old blonde on his arm when he hit sixty, just to make other men envious. And so he did. The woman just laughs. She was tired of him anyway. The only thing that bothers her is that he owes her twenty thousand dollars from the divorce settlement, and so does Maynard's stepfather. She kept the house where Darla was raised, where Maynard was brought as a baby, where Matt visited once, where you, Billy, used to come visit your son. Halfway through the breakfast, her "killer abs" flat as pancakes, swell, and she offers the rest to Maynard, who has eyed her plate from the beginning as he wolfed down his omelette and toast. He eagerly mops up every morsel, the way you did at a restaurant, hungry as a wolf. He seems to inhale the food and still hold his nose to the air for more.

THE FRENCH WAITRESS is highly stressed and old. She has waited on us with a curt manner, noticeably irritated by the tableful of "Italians." With an European eye, she has calculated the ethnicity and dealt accordingly. Her voice changes from table to table depending on the "nationality." Your father shows her the same hidden contempt she shows his rough, demanding ordering off the menu. He has made special requests to hold this and add that, which she gets mixed up and forgets one order altogether. He doesn't hide his disapproval. His face is twisted up, and he bats at the air, as if to shoo away a gnat. The grandson gets a big kick out of his antics again. He turns to his mother each time to catch her eye, and they laugh and laugh at the old man, the new grandpa. The Italian. The kid is learning to be Italian. It is what he wanted to do since leaving the rich Jewish stepfather. Now he's got a male model. All he has to do is be rude and loud and directive, learn the waitress's first name, get all cozy with her, and ask for special privileges, as if they're family already. She brings cayenne in a dish, fresh basil chopped up for the herb seasoning on the no-yolk eggs, and fresh coffee as often as possible. She's finally run ragged, and the smile is a grimace when she brings the bill. She fears your father finding a mistake, but he does. He calls her over and taps his old finger over her scrawled abreviations and asks what it is. She has to hover and figure out that it was one of the sides Darla ordered. At last he digs into his wallet and lays out the dollar bills, gnashing his dentures all the while. And breakfast is over.

OUTSIDE, THE SUNSHINE is weak but burning off the fog. The ocean is just over there beyond those housing tracts. The day's plans are made. Maynard will come back to the motel with us, and Darla and her daughter and the dog will go home and continue packing. We will all meet for supper at some place. They will let her know. The treat again is your dad's. It's understood. They owe Darla seventeen years of dinners.

SO SHE SOUP-ENGINES IT off in her Porsche, the dog's ears and her hair blowing in the wind. What a mom. A super mom. A stylish mom. The Goddess mom. It's in all the handbooks for women today. "You are a goddess," it tells women, and cites historical women and mythical women to plump up their theory. And women like Darla believe it and act accordingly. A goddess first, woman second, sex symbol, lover, and mother. All the roles, as long as you can live them with your rich ex-husband's alimony check in style. Her kids are dazzled by her. They are in love with her. She is the epitome of the image of the fashionable Hollywood image. Like Nicole Simpson. She is status. Such a mom. And she has her thirty-nine year old energies, is in love with a thirty-year- old fireman. What a hunk. His neck will be as thick as his head, we will soon see for ourselves over dinner. She is due to pick him up at the airport in the early afternoon.

BACK AT THE MOTEL, everyone mills about, planning the day, drinking water from the salty breakfast, deciding who and where, what and when. They've got the grandson for the first time. A grandson for the very first time, and now how to entertain him is on their mind. They don't ask him what he wants to do. They don't give away their power. He is still a kid, and they will decide what they want to do and he must go along with them. He is polite and doesn't make any demands. But he is not shy. They turn on the game and he begins to shout and cheer along with your mother, father, and brother. Your mother takes note of this and buries her eyes into tissues. He sounds just like you did. He likes the same team, the same

142

players. He knows what you know about sports. They ask him questions and it breaks your mother's heart. Your brother marvels. Your father takes it for granted. How many sports choices does anyone have anyway is on his face. Sure, the kid's no dummy. The kid laughs at your old man's attitude again and again. Your dad doubles up his fist and mocks punching him out. They both laugh and laugh. And then everyone goes out the door to stroll along the harbor. There's an art and crafts show going on. That will be something to do. The boy is like a trained bear on an invisible chain. He walks obediently along as if he is interested. It is obvious to any by-stander that he has a salacious side and would just as soon be off getting all he could in physical sensation with his peers than to accompany these new grandparents along the wharf in such a conventional manner. The day wears away and they take him home to clean up for dinner as his mother requested. Your family returns to the motel and rests to prepare for the evening out. Your mother takes off her shoes and Matt instructs her to elevate her feet and close her eyes and try to meditate. He instructs your father to take off his shoes and wear his earth shoes with the rubber bumps inside to stimulate his sole. And to hold off on the hors d'oeuvres, and definitely not to drink any wine if he is going to have some with dinner. They do as he says, your mother sighing, and your father frowning as if brow- beaten by this son. They flip on the television and find the channel they want and then go about their business preparing for the evening with the live T.V. screen as background. Matt goes with Eme to their room and turns the T.V. on immediately and sits back on the bed focussing on it. Eme kicks off her shoes, jumps in the shower, scalds herself to rid herself of all the slow-moving, polite talk, and generally being out of place with this family. She comes out of the steam, refreshed and drowsy and falls into a nice sleep between the silky sheets, groaning with the creature comforts Matt has provided by getting this pretty room. She has covered her head with a pillow to drown out the sound of the television.

DINNER TONIGHT IS AT AN ITALIAN PLACE. The menu is big and stiff and covered with choices at family prices. Your parents and Matt and Eme arrive ahead of time to case the joint. They want to check it out to see if it is suitable for the new relatives. Tonight Darla's fiancé will be there. We have heard all about what "a hunk" he is. We've heard about how he got his ear knocked off when a firehose went wild on one job he had. How he had to have a nerve cut so that his balance wouldn't be off. He was walking sideways and laying his head over parallel to the ground. After that he was able to walk straight up, but could no longer be a fireman. Now he's landed a job as a paramedic. This is the man the mother of your son has in her life right now. Your parents don't let on that they are at all interested. After all, the time for you to be her mate is long gone. And the way she goes on about his size, would make their son, you, seem like a midget. Your father comes to Darla's shoulders. Her legs are most of her height, so that he is almost eye-level to her small breasts. He has to look up all the time, talking with this new family. Even your son dwarfs your father, and would have stood a head higher than you. Matt comes to his shoulders. Your short parents walk around the premises, read

144

the menu, and then make the call to tell everyone to come down. They take a long table in the large diningroom and sit and wait, reading the menu to pass the time. Eme takes a walk. She is restauranted out. All the sitting has gotten her antsy. She makes her way around the shopping center and then circles the restaurant and watches your parents wait. Then she sees the guests arrive. There's Darla and her lover, your son, her young daughter, her mother. They get out of her new van, the one the rich Jew bought her before his stroke, and stride across the parking lot to the restaurant. Your mother's niece and her husband park and are making their way toward the restaurant, too. He's the one who picked up the tab last night. He's the one who always tells the waiter it's his birthday, sitting there grinning. Eme waits until everyone is seated, and then reluctantly enters. She is tired of eating as a pastime and a medium of socializing. Matt is seated and begins greetings all around. A tableful of people is his speciality. He loves the gatherings on behalf of you and your parents. There can't be enough recognition paid to your parents in this respect. Darla avoids your parents' end of the table and seats herself by Eme. She introduces Bud all around. Smiles, salutations, joviality. Maynard centers himself so that both ends of the long table have access to him, the old folks down at your parents end and the younger ones up at his mother's end. He's ready for the big feed again. Bud keeps an eye on him, as if he is in charge of all that young male energy. Bud only 30 and Maynard 17. Hardly a father figure, but he can match young male antics and tactics for young male antics and tactics. Bud's suddenly the "mature" man who's been through all the stages Maynard is going through. And everyone can see what Darla is up to. She can't handle Maynard alone anymore and she wants Bud to take over. Word will soon get out slowly that Maynard was sent off to, not only a private high school in Northern California, but one for problem kids. Drugs and alcohol, petty crime, family problems. Bud looks hell bent to get the kid in line, having heard all the horror stories of his street days. He seems outraged that the kid could have given his girlfriend, Darla, such a bad time. There is a certain determination in his manner with Maynard that tells of wanting to show Darla how he will straighten everything out once and for all. He will prove to her that he may be young, but he is big and he is a man.

DINNER IS ANOTHER SESSION of the waiters lining up and singing Happy Birthday to your mother's niece's husband. They bring him a piece of cake with a candle in it, and we all laugh, half embarrassed, because, of course it is not his birthday again. The old people talk and the younger people talk, and then everyone bids goodnight. Darla hangs onto Bud, her long arms and legs aching to cling to him like a big teddy bear. We can all feel her urgency to be held by him all night long. They've been separated a week. Maynard ignores his mother's ardor for this young man. Later, he will move out of their house in Sacramento, telling Matt that he couldn't take their sexual innuendos any longer. Watching your mother love-sick over some big hunk who is bossing you around and taking ownership of her, will prove to be too much. And Darla will go along. What does she know. She

146

loves Bud, and she is not to miss out on him just because her son is having growing pains and wants to challenge the brute. She comes first, as always, as you recall way back then. In 1978, she did what she wanted, too.

THE NEXT DAY MATT DECIDES that they will move to another motel. Eme points out that $95 a night twice is exorbitant, not that it is any of her business. And there is a Ramada Inn advertising rooms at $59 a night. She points to a big sign as they drive by. So your family makes the move from the Travel Lodge, much to the grumbling of your father over to the Ramada Inn, which is just down the block. He doesn't care about saving a hundred dollars. It's just one more night anyway. He likes the first motel. Matt made reservations over the phone from home without comparing prices. But he packs up, methodically putting everything into the trunk of his car and then unpacks at the new place, carrying baggage like a burro, one tedious step at a time. Right away, your mother notices that the new place is owned by Koreans, and that the carpet in the entranceway is shabby and stained. She looks past it, though, and goes along with the plan.

A BIG KOREAN MAN in baggy black slacks and a slack mouth who doesn't smile, takes your mother's bags and puts them in the elevator. Again you mother notices some lack of maintenance but says nothing. On the second floor your father tries the key. It doesn't work. He squawks like a goose. Your mother stands there fuming into her blouse. Matt runs down the stairs to the office and reports this. Soon a young Korean girl with a tool belt appears. She is pretty and all smiles in jeans and a men's t-shirt. She laughs it away, as if it's a joke and opens the door with her key and then demonstrates how your father is to place the "key" which is a card into the slot and then when it is at a certain point, turn the door knob. Your parents are exhausted by this incident. They are accompanied into their room by your brother, who reaches to turn on the lamp. There is no bulb in the lamp. Matt goes into a desperation gesture, wiping his face and punching the air. But this is just the beginning. Before the night is over, your mother will make out a list of sixteen things that didn't work. The miniblind will not have a rod to open and close with, and it is visibly missing one of the blinds, like a mouth with one tooth out. On first glance the rooms looked nice. But as your family reaches for handles and knobs, switches and flushers, they will find them loose and wobbly or non-existent. Eme has gone to her room and delights in their being a jet blower jacuzzi in the bathtub. There is a switch on the wall that turns it on. The instructions list the steps, and she reads them aloud when Matt comes back to the room and flops on the bed sighing with disgust over the place, ranting that one would think a Ramada Inn would be up to standards. And then remembers that he read somewhere that they can be bought and owned independently now. He holds his tongue about the lower standards of some peoples. Eme is in the bathroom trying to place a plug into the drain as the instructions says. It won't go in and when she turns on the faucets, the tub drains. Matt gets on the phone and calls the office again, and in a deadpan voice, like the Mafia, insinuates that the proper plug should be brought to the room immediately. This time an obese woman with red hair and rowdy-dowdy western jeans and plaid shirt appears. She strains to bend down and insert the plug the right way. So, for the rest of the evening, Eme jacuzzis, Matt catches the commentary of the O.J. trial and who knows what your parents do. They must sleep in a queen-sized bed with a wedding canopy at the head, attached to the ceiling.

YOUR MOTHER IGNORES this bit of romantic decor while your father bellows, "We're just married," and shakes his shaggy head like an old goat.

THE NEXT MORNING Eme wants the free breakfast of orange juice and pastry and coffee. Matt will not allow your parents to go near it. And by the time Eme gets there, everything has been put away. The big Korean man goes into the back room and brings the orange juice out of the refrigerator. The obese girl, still in western dress, has said a definite, "No, it's only "til ten." Eme gulps down a couple of paper cupsful and then reads the label. All from concentrate fortified with corn syrup. Matt laughs. What did she expect? Your parents glance at her, control their smirks, and shake their heads.

THE CAR IS PACKED. The plan today is to drive by Darla's, say goodbye to everyone and go home. Matt is eager, as is your mother and father. It's the end of a long emotional uniting with your past, after just burying you a week ago. The only fly in the ointment is that Eme mentioned that since they were going north, and the other grandmother lived just off the freeway, that they would surely give her a ride home so she wouldn't have to take the train. Jewell has made Eme promise to sit by her and talk to her the whole way, so she herself won't have to talk. Your mother wanted to cry all the way home and now she will not be able to do that for at least forty-five minutes until they drop off Renée. Renée, the other grandmother, has taken a liking to Eme who has nothing at stake and speaks the truth of the matter as she sees it, so complies with not trying to engage your mother in conversation.

THEY ARE ALL WAITING to say goodbye. Bud is in the garage taking the last piece of Darla's gym apart and guiding the movers just how to pack it in the big Mayflower Moving and Storage truck parked at curbside. Darla looks well-sexed and softened for the move up north with her honey. Hugs all around and bids of farewell with only goodwill. But in a couple of months, Matt will report to Eme that she never called once, and neither did the grandmother. They had to make all the overtures of staying in touch. This makes sense to Eme. She tells Matt that your parents must be the ones to come hat-in-hand and woo this family. That after your mother giving Renée the cold shoulder all the way up the coast, and your father wanting to just drop her and her bag off in the driveway and be

150

on his way, she doesn't doubt why you were able to leave your infant son behind seventeen years ago. She points out that your parents are "bothered" by doing the little kindnesses, and then they expect this family to kiss their arses and pursue them. No way, man. Eme gets belligerent. Matt listens, silent, as usual.

ONCE HOME, THEY REFLECT ON the trip ever so briefly. Well, they have a grandson now. What does that mean? What do you do now? They will call every Sunday at five o'clock. They want him to come to a big family clan birthday party Lydia and Hugh are throwing for ninety-year-old Mark. He can meet everyone. He wants to be Italian, this is where he can learn how it's done. They laugh about that. Your mother shows photos to Isabel. They marvel over how much he looks like you. Your mother creates a little altar affair on one bureau top. Your picture next to your son's picture. And some trinket that you had and one he gave them. She sniffles as she passes it. She will have her good days and her bad days is the way she will put it as time goes on. Your son cannot come to the big family party. It interferes with school. Bud and Darla tell him to move out if he doesn't like listening to their smooching in the evenings in front of T.V. Six months will pass and they will have sent him a hundred dollars for his birthday. They will have enjoyed how he calls them "Grandma and Grandpa," and asks, "What's happening?" But they will have no plan to see him, put off by the fact that his mother wouldn't let him skip school for a once-in-a lifetime-family party of all your relatives. They will have a grandson by name only. And so it goes. Your mother grieves your death just as hard, and takes some enjoyment talking to Maynard once a week. But she has told everyone, "Now I have another heartache, if anything should happen to Maynard."

YOUR FATHER IS TURNING 80 today. You were due home the day before yesterday on June 8th. Your mother trembled over the date. She was afraid for it to be June 8th. Your brother knew this. He began watching her. She knew he was watching her. Some people don't remember when tragedy hits. Others use the date as a time of dread, as if one day could be worse than another once someone is dead. "A reminder," your mother says. She had such plans. A reunion and birthday party in one to celebrate your return and your father's eightieth. It's been five months. That's a long time and it's not very long, depending on who's talking to your family. Some people expect them to get on with their lives, and others know how hard it is, and still others understand your family and know they don't have much else to hang onto. Your parents retired and your brother not having to work. Everyone lounging around the apartment. You were their focus, their purpose, their direction. What you were doing was always on their minds because you were the only one doing anything. You refused to sit around the house with them and keep the family intact. Matt was always mad at you for not calling every day and every night to report on your whereabouts and your daily activities, and to say goodnight. You refused, saying you were a forty-year- old man, not some teenager. Now your death takes the place of your life, and they create all the same purpose, focus, and direction around it. Matt confesses to Eme that he is amazed that your death has given him a reason to get up in the morning. Now he knows what his life is all about, where before he was free floating. His life has taken shape around you, still. He's built a structure, a routine, a vigorous thought process around sleuthing your death, and intellectualizing it, and placing it in the right order, so as to have it like an object he can turn and study and "have." He has you now. He knows the outcome. It has narrowed his eyes in amazement over reality. He marvels over his former naïveté. How he didn't know this was coming, and how it came and who he is now because of it. He never calls it self-discovery. He puts it into a religious realm and goes to the priest to ask him what to think of it.

YOUR MOTHER IS TAKEN OUT TO DINNER now on Thursday nights at 5:50 to The Natural Cafe to eat before her appointment at Hospice. Mr. Pugh is still sitting there waiting for your mother to spill her guts; but she prefers to have him give an educational lecture on the theory behind the grieving process. She and Matt are "thinkers." They don't like to feel their feelings, and both have done a good job avoiding them all their lives, except for the anger Matt lets go on you, and the anxiety, which is your mother's emotion of choice, if she had to pinpoint one. And the suppressed anger which Matt has identified as "passive aggression." A meek person's revenge. She shut down years ago when she found out her life was not going to be what she thought it would. But, what was that? No one ever asked her how she planned her life and how it turned out, and how she turned sour and went about her duties like an obedient slave, who had her little ways of "getting even." She doesn't know enough about herself to talk to Pugh about this. She believes what you said at their 50th wedding anniversary: "My mother is the most loving person in this whole world, bar none. There is not a kinder person than my mother. She shows love for everyone. She has never said a bad word about anyone, and I mean ever." You said it on television, too, one Mother's day, when the T.V. camera was on you and a microphone held out. The man on the street. What does he think of his mother.

MATT INVITES EME TO JOIN your mother and him at The Natural that evening of June 7th. Your mother puts her hand up to guard her mouth as she speaks these words to Eme, "Tomorrow, Billy was suppose to come home. I'm very nervous about it." Eme looks blank and thinks she is talking about your father, Billy, coming home and asks if he has been away, or in the hospital, or what? Your mother looks downright hateful, searching her face to see if she is kidding. She sees that Eme is confused. "You know, my Billy, in Australia." Oh, Eme finally gets the point. She goes silent. What can one say to a mother who has awaited the date of your return with such fear. Your mother turns to Matt and says, "Matti, call and find out the schedule of that flight in from Australia. There's one a day. And see if Billy is on it. Maybe this whole thing is a hoax. Maybe he is coming home."

MATT SAYS NOTHING. Eme winces. It is a poignant moment. The words stay in the air and cause their pain. She wants you to come off that plane so bad it hurts. It hurts so bad, like that throat-wrenching song that came out fifteen years before. It is at the sidewalk cafe tables with the late summer sun warming them that they retreat into their own thoughts after your mother's words. They eat the health food mechanically. Tomorrow is the big day when you won't ever be coming home again. The guy they sent was you. It wasn't a mannikin. You weren't playing a practical joke like in the movies. Your mother sacrifices half her veggie plate to Matt, who has swallowed his whole and sits eyeing hers. He takes hers and wolfs it down, too. Your mother is bothered by food anymore. She used to relish every bite. Now it is simply necessary to eat to stay alive. She doesn't care to enjoy it since you can't. A big dog thrusts his face near your mother's elbow and eyes her plate, moving his eyebrows in the way dogs do to follow the movements of humans hoping for a bite of their food. Your mother turns and asks, "Who are you? You're no one to us. Go away." She scoffs. Eme says, "Oh, it's a doggy." And she puts her plate on the floor under the table for him to lick. Matt laughs as your mother looks alarmed. Later, Eme will tell Matt that his mother is cruel. If that dog had belonged to someone in the family, then she'd feed it, but if it's just a dog, she can easily turn away. Matt says nothing at all. It would not occur to him either to feed a dog that no one knew. So much for your mother being "the kindest person in the whole world," as you announced during their 50th wedding anniversary. Eme says, "She only has an absence of unkindness, not an active kindness." Your brother lets it land on deaf ears.

YOUR MOTHER WANTS TO have a nice dinner out for your father's Eightieth. She makes calls to old Isabel and Mark, Lydia and Hugh, and Eme, and Norma, the neighbor who has been so thoughtful with her gifts on the porch weekly, and her calls and attention. Norma, with the wide good teeth, even at her age, a smile a mile long, and white, but with spaces in between, so they have to be real. Would a dentist make such dentures? The dinner turns into a breakfast. Because you are not going to be here, your father will not tolerate a big bash of a dinner for his birthday. He will agree to a light breakfast and then your mother and he will go to the graveyard and sit and talk to you for awhile. And so it is. Everyone comes. Old Mark is a token of his former self. Rotund as a beachball in his slacks and shirt, with Isabel shrinking beside him. He is wearing her out with incontinence, diapers, eating, dressing, any daily activity. He is now a two hundred pound infant, and she shrivels under the load of taking care of him.

STILL HIS SONS WOULD NOT ALLOW for her to get a day nurse. This is their father, and what's a wife for? Their mother's job is to take care of him until the end. Mark never speaks, and Isabel can't hear anymore, so they are fine at a tableful of people. Your parents scowl and frown. They demonstrate how they have to go through the motions of having a birthday celebration for your dad at 80, but that they will not enjoy it a bit. Lydia and Hugh are their sparkling selves, as if sprinkled with fairy dust. Both silver-white haired and tanned from Mexico getaways, in their red, white, and blue true American sports clothes. They keep the conversation lively and laughable. They will not match the tone of the birthday boy. Your dad is mostly silent and glaring out of his blue eyes. He glowers around the table as he mops up the maple syrup with his buckwheat cakes, as if he challenges anyone to be happy on a day when you are not here. It finally become tiresome. Everyone wants your parents to get over it. Or else not try to celebrate anything if they have to come and show their grim faces. Eme leaves first. She has family in town. She has fallen into the mock hugging and kissing at the sides of the faces that this big Italian family does. She bids everyone farewell and breathes a sigh of relief. She is always fuming over the way your family is. Now she recognizes what your sighs and silences were all about.

SO, THAT WAS THE CELEBRATION you were suppose to be included in. Instead you lie dead. After breakfast, your parents go on over and spread out their straw beach mats and sit down on your grave. Who knows what they say. Matt has never ventured near the cemetery. He has never looked at a photograph of you. He wants no reminders. As if knowing you are dead isn't a reminder enough. Eme has asked him what he would do if he watched the video tape she made of you the night before you left for Australia. He didn't answer her. And one night, while she was watching an old family tape of hers, you suddenly appeared on the screen. Matt threw his hands over his eyes and ran outside into the night to get out of her room. She laughed. "But you know he is dead. Why can't you SEE him. Don't you want to study him?" He refused to come back until the tape was finished, but she coaxed him back in, saying that was the only part with you on it. As she spoke, there you were again. Again he covered his eyes and ran from the room. Again she laughed and asked why. Again he never answered.

OH, BILLY, if you'd just come home as planned you would have fit back into the picture and things would be just the way they always were, everyone worrying about you but getting by and not knowin' from nothin'. This way, it hurts so bad. It hurts so bad....

A Beta Book

ARE YOU A BUDDING AUTHOR? You've written a book manuscript—now what? Two new factors have revolutionized publishing.

1. The cost of printing review copies has plummeted to nearly nothing.

2. The rest of publishing—editorial, design, illustration—is turning into a cottage industry.

Given those two factors, *you can make your own publishing decisions.*

Consult the Beta Books site (www.betabooks. us) to find and hire (or not) your own proof-reader, editor, critiquer, reviewer, designer, illustrator, marketer. You are in control.

The typical Beta Book project is to provide you with enough ARCs (Advance Reading Copies) for reviewers or distributors, so you can start the buzz about your book, and get the word out.

—www.betabooks.us—